Road agent Comanche John never had an argument he couldn't win with a Colt—until he contracted to guide a rag-tag bunch of farmers across the Rocky Ranges.

Lawford Hames was out to get Comanche—and the wagon train. He had gold, men, and the law on his side. He thought they added up to a match for The Fastest Gun.

THE FASTEST GUN

Dan Cushman

GUNSMOKE

This hardback edition 2004
by BBC Audiobooks Ltd
by arrangement with
Golden West Literary Agency

ISBN 0 7540 8263 6

British Library Cataloguing in Publication Data available.

Printed and bound in Great Britain by
Antony Rowe Ltd., Chippenham, Wiltshire

CHAPTER ONE

THERE WAS A BITE OF WINTER in the air, making the black-whiskered man shiver and draw his buckskin jacket more snugly around his shoulders. He pulled his slouch hat down, too, and he scrooched a trifle over the neck of his gunpowder roan pony, all without taking his eyes off the mountain valley below.

The valley lay lifeless. Not even a deer was browsing. The spruce timber was green-purple-black, the brush was tinted ruddy from frost, and the river, the Lemhi, had a flat shine, like metal.

The black-whiskered man was patient. He waited for more than an hour. At last a rider appeared, cantering warily as befitted a white man in that year of 1863, rifle across the pommel of his saddle. He climbed his horse to a small promontory and had a long look at the valley ahead. Satisfied, he turned and signaled with wide sweeps of his hat. A canvas-topped wagon soon appeared, and then others. It was an emigrant train, apparently the one the black-whiskered man was waiting for, because at last he moved, grunting satisfaction, and sending out a long spurt of tobacco juice.

"Yep, thar she be," he said. "That's the Parson's wagon." He squinted far down at a wagon top with words lettered on it in black paint: *REPENT YE FOR THE DAY OF JUDGMENT IS AT HAND.* "I wish I knew what that says, but it's gospel talk. Yep, it be. That's the Parson. They made it nigh on schedule."

Still, he was in no hurry. His way of life had taught him to be wary, and always have a second or third look before showing himself. He took time now to scratch all through his whiskers. His age could have been anywhere from 35 to 45. His skin was browned the hue of saddle leather. He was shorter than average, and somewhat broader, a breadth accentuated by his long-stirruped manner of sitting a horse. His hat was a black slouch sombrero, his jacket was squaw-made with here and there some beadwork, although most of it had been torn away by brush. His trousers were gray homespun; he wore jackboots pulled up to protect his knees from the brush that grew thickly in those Idaho mountains. Around his waist on crossed belts was a brace of Colts, Navy model, cap and ball, caliber .36.

The scout rode down and commenced signaling the wagons into a circle. The first arrivals started a fire. Cooking utensils commenced to appear, and on the breeze came odors that made the whiskered man's stomach go bottomless from hunger, so he delayed no longer, but gave rein to his pony and started picking his way downward across the rocks and deadfalls that strewed the ridge. "That's the wagon train," he said. "That cooking *does* smell like Christian folk."

Timber closed in on him. He could no longer see the camp, but its sounds came to him—the axes cutting wood, the raised voices, the clattering of pans. Then he heard a banjo and a flexible tenor voice, slightly na-sal but a good voice for all of that—and the song! Yes, the song! It made him sit straight with appreciation.

For the whiskered man was Comanche John, and the song was about himself:

> *"Oh, gather 'round, ye teamster men,*
> *   And listen to my tale,"*

sang the nasal tenor,

> *"Of the worst side-windin' varmint*
> *   That rides the outlaw trail;*
> *He wears the name Comanche John*
> *   And he comes from old Missou,*
> *Where many a Concord coach he stopped*
> *   And many a gun he drew."*

"Rusty," somebody bellowed. "Quit singing and

fetch some water."

The banjo stopped, and another man said, "Aw, let him sing, Lafe. I'll fetch the water. I think I'd of gone crazy already if it hadn't been for his singin' and banjoin'."

"Well, tell him to sing something besides that road-agent doggerel."

Comanche John then emerged from timber. He was in full view of the camp, but though this was Indian country, *bad* Indian country with the Nez Percé renegades on the prowl, nobody paid the slightest attention to him.

He crossed a level bench where grass grew to the knees of his pony and drew up between a couple of supply wagons, the early darkness at his back, with firelight just reaching him.

"Hello," he said, and several men stopped what they were doing to look at him, surprised now, knowing he was a stranger.

"That war a beautiful piece." He addressed the banjo player, a tall, skinny, redheaded fellow of about nineteen. "And ye have a fine voice for it, too. Ye could turn a good wage with that voice singing in the music halls over around Bannock on the Montana side, I'm thinking. Have ye ever heered *this* verse to that song?" And tuning his voice he sang:

"Comanche rode to Yallerjack
  In the year of sixty-two,
With Three-Gun-Bob and Dillon
  And a man named Henry Drew;
They robbed the stage, they robbed the bank,
  They robbed the Western mail;
And many a cheek did blanch to hear
  Their names spoke on the trail."

"I never heard that one!" the young man said eagerly, chording his banjo. "If you—"

"Git to work," shouted the man called Lafe. "Damn it, sing after supper." He was short, powerful, and good-natured. "Ahoy, stranger," he said to John. "You look like you'd traveled a piece. You come from the Yallerstone? Come from the gold fields?"

"I come from a heap o' places both near and far. I be a weary pilgrim." He sat smelling the cooking. "A Christian man. Share and share alike, that's my motto."

Men were coming as the word traveled that a stranger from the gold fields of Montana country was in camp. He watched them. He did not dismount. He sat slouched to one side, a posture that brought the butt of his right-hand Navy Colt away from his hip; he chawed sleepily; he yawned, but his eyes were ever narrow and alert.

He asked, "Be they one amongst ye by the handle of the Reverend Jeremiah Parker?"

A big, red-whiskered man said, "The Parson?" He walked close up with a heavy-booted, tired man's limp. "Say, are you the guide that was to meet us at Fort Hall?"

"Now. I might be, but I didn't promise to meet ye at Fort Hall. The Parson said Fort Hall or the Lemhi, and this be the Lemhi."

"Well," the big man said, rubbing his chin, "you're welcome to light and have grub, but I guess we got over needing a guide."

Comanche John said mildly, "I rode five-six sleeps across some mighty rough country to meet this train and guide it to the Bitterroot, and whilst I'm in favor of an outfit being able to change its mind, on t'other hand I don't like it to be quite that free with my time." He spat and added, "And my horse don't, neither."

Lafe said to the red-whiskered one, "Listen, Stocker, that was never put to a vote."

Stocker, rearing his shoulders up in a bull-moose posture, shouted, "Dammit, no matter what he says, he was to meet us at Fort Hall! He changed his mind, so now we can change our'n. I say he's late and we don't need him."

"Let's take it up with Wood."

"We don't *need* to take it up with Wood."

Comanche John dismounted. He limped around getting the stiffness from his joints. "I ain't the man I used to be," he muttered, "I ain't, for a fact. I'm going to find me a squaw and settle down."

They had sent for the Reverend Jeremiah Parker. The Reverend came at a half-lope, a spare old man with wispy gray hair that fell over his shoulders, a shaved face, and a neck like a plucked rooster's. Behind him was a kid of fifteen trying to get him to put on a black greatcoat.

"John!" cried the Reverend Parker, stopping and stretching his arms half toward the black-whiskered man and half toward the heavens. "*John!* I told 'em you'd come. I prayed. And all the while I could feel the power of those prayers like a rope dragging you across those mountains."

"If ye don't mind," said John. "I'd just as leaf you didn't mention that word *rope*. All over Montana the only thing folks wanted to talk about was rope."

The Parson came closer, staring at him with his protruding eyeballs. He came close to say quietly, "John, you ain't tooken to your old ways!"

"I'm innocent as a babe unborn, and might' nigh as bankrupt. I given up the ways of sin and its wages, too. May I be struck with lightning if I had my hand in a single robbery except for maybe one coach, and that because it had Union money on it, an act of war, me being a Confederate."

"Well—" said the Parson and decided to let it pass. "What name you going by?"

"Smith. Sometimes I call myself Jones, and sometimes Brown, but generally just plain Smith. It's not so unusual, attracts less attention."

"Hush!" said the Parson. "Here comes trouble."

A very handsome, well-built man of about 35 was just walking up in the strong light of the fire. He was not an ordinary wagoner. There was something of the aristocrat in his bearing. He was dressed in antelope-skin breeches and shirt, and a very wide-brimmed beaver hat. The garb was ordinary enough on the frontier, but his air and body gave it quality. Around his waist, buckled high, was a new Army .44 and a patent powder, ball, and cap dispenser. A whip, its long lash rolled in a neat circle, had been thrust in his belt. His eyes were on John. He nodded. There was a cold courtesy in his smile.

"This be John Smith," said the Parson.

"Hames," the man said. "I'm Lawford Hames. I'm guiding the wagon train. I'm sorry if there was some misunderstanding."

"I doubt they's been one."

Hames still smiled, but it became colder. He offered to shake hands. "You were to meet them at Fort Hall. You weren't there. I happened to be, so I took the job."

"Lucky for us," said Stocker. "Hames was a mighty big freighter down in Coloraydo."

John said, "All the way from Colorado to guide an emigrant train. This is pretty decent of you, Hames."

"It's what I choose to do," said Hames.

As if to drive this home, he came down hard on John's hand, showing his strength, and he was very strong. Caught unawares, it seemed to John that the bones in his hand were being ground to splinters.

John did not try to free himself. He simply placed a foot on Hames's toe and nudged him backward. Hames found himself unbalanced. He tried to drop John's hand and get clear. John had him, both hands on the wrist. John bent double, bringing his arm over his shoulder in an Indian whip lock. Hames's feet were jerked clear of the ground, his abdomen borne by John's shoulders, and next instant he was deposited in a sprawled position, on his back, on the ground.

He lay for half a second in shock. His hat rolled off. His hair was knocked over his eyes. He recovered and twisted over then, with a quickness surprising for one of his size, and his right hand went for the .44 Army Colt, but Comanche John, with a casual, hitching movement, had already unholstered his left-hand Navy.

Hames froze. His mouth was slightly open. He did not breathe. The gun muzzle held him hypnotized. It was so quiet for the space of three or four seconds that one could hear the snap of logs in the big cookfire.

"Now that trick," said John, "I learnt off'n the Comanches, whose specialty is wrestling. And if ye ever try to strong-hand me again I'll show you a trick I learnt from Wild Bill Graves, whose specialty was shooting men right betwixt the eyes."

Hames took his hand away from his gun. Still staring at the Navy, making every move slowly, like one who has awakened with a rattlesnake coiled by his bed and fears to startle it, he got his hands behind him and climbed to his feet.

"Thar," said John. "That's the ticket. I'm not looking to shoot anybody. 'The meek shall inherit the earth.' I'm a man of religious leanings myself. Yea, I am a stranger amongst ye with my back turned on the gulch of sin, and that's straight from the psalms of David, it is for a fact." And he holstered his Navy.

Hames struggled for his composure. He was furious. He was hollow-eyed and hollow-cheeked from fury. The muscles stood out at the sides of his jaw and the veins on his forehead. He had a hard time getting words to come through his taut lips: "You— Get out! I'm warning you, get out of this camp!"

John chawed, and spat, and moved back just a trifle. He was wary for someone behind him. When John made no move to leave, Hames swung around on the stunned wagoners.

"Tell him to leave. You hired me as a guide. Is this the kind of support you give the man who offered to guide you through the mountains?"

The men looked at one another and shifted uncomfortably. They were roughly dressed men, farming men, most of them approaching middle years. They had been uprooted by war and poverty and were having the struggle of their lives merely keeping their families going without mixing in gun fights.

Then big, red-whiskered Stocker said, "Yes, he's right, what kind of support is this, letting this stranger come in camp, start throwing men over his back, wave guns around—"

"If you ask me, you had it coming!"

It was the raw voice of a woman. She was gangling tall, her height accentuated by a high-waisted calico dress which she held up with one hand to keep from catching grass and twigs as she walked. On her head was a long poke bonnet. Strapped around her waist was a double-barreled shot pistol, once a flintlock, now converted to percussion, a massive blunderbuss that weighed at least five pounds.

She stopped. She looked at Hames. She despised him. She looked at Stocker. There were some other men who had just come hurrying up from the brush along the river. She despised them just as she did Hames, because they were his men. Comanche John could tell they were his men. He could tell by their guns and by the way they carried themselves. And anyway, he could tell by the way this woman looked at them.

She yelled, "Yes, you had it coming, Hames. Always showing off how strong you are, making like to bust the bones in a man's hand. You did it to Rusty once. That, or showing off with your whip. Knocking the pipes out of men's mouths with your whip! You'll put somebody's eye out one of these days with that whip. But finally you run into your match!" Then she turned her attention to John. "Praise be to glory, did I hear you ejaculate that you were a religious man?"

"I hit the sawdust trail," said John piously, with his thumbs hooked in his gun belts. "I turned my back on Rocky Bar, which is worse'n Sodom, and on Bannock City, which is nigh as bad as Gomorrah. I'm a pilgrim on the trail o' life. I been buffeted by fate, and chased by the minions of the unrighteous."

"Glory Amen!"

A trifle sourly, the red-whiskered Stocker said, "I

hate to bring this up, Betsy, but he *does* seem to be a trifle weighted down with Sam Colt metal for a sky pilot."

"And why wouldn't he be, the company he has to keep? Tell me this, stranger, do ye believe in baptism by total immersion, or are you just a hair dipper?"

"I be a Methodist till I die!"

"Well," said Betsty with a slight diminution of enthusiasm, "I guess that'll have to do."

A small, middle-aged man had that moment ridden up and dismounted, and the crowd opened for him. He walked up, thin from the trail, but still carrying himself with vigor.

Betsy said, "Thar's Wood! Now we got somebody with *sense.*"

"What's the excitement?" Wood asked. It was evident that this man rather than the noisy Stocker was their leader. Betsy started to answer, but he shook his head and indicated that he wanted to hear from Stocker.

Stocker said, "Why, *this* is the Parson's guide. He just showed up. Rode in out of the night. Two weeks late."

Wood said, "He made no agreement to meet us in Fort Hall, if that's what you mean. I've tried to tell you that. The Parson *asked* him to meet us there, otherwise here on the Lemhi. Well, here he is. This is the Lemhi."

Stocker, scratching around at his tangled red hair, muttered, "Damn it, I say he should o' been in Fort Hall. Gettin' his money easy showing *here* instead of Fort Hall."

Hames cried, "You hired me. I'm guiding the train. I have an agreement!"

Wood said, "I've told you several times that I intend to take no bullyragging."

A girl, a very pretty, dark-haired girl of seventeen or eighteen, had followed Wood into the light. A similarity in their manners revealed them to be father and daughter.

"Ambrose," she said, staring at Hames in surprise, "what's the matter with you?"

"Sorry." He got control of himself. There were fragments of grass and twigs on his beaver hat, and on his soft-rubbed antelope-skin shirt. He brushed himself off and fingered his wavy hair back into place. "I was just surprised to see your dad take the attitude he did. You know very well the agreement we had."

The Parson started in on him, magpie-voiced, long-armed, and wild-haired, only to be checked by Wood, who said, "Never mind, Parson. Save it for Sunday. Right now we're all tired and hungry. We'll have a full meeting on it after supper. Anger never settled anything. And anger isn't *going* to settle anything, not here, not while I'm captain. Not ever!"

CHAPTER TWO

THE CROWD BROKE UP into smaller groups which had their own private talk. Many cooked at the big fire and then ate by themselves at their own wagons, but there were several other cookfires: outside, in the shelter of river banks and trees, or inside the wagons which had little emigrant stoves set up.

Comanche John, with his back propped against a wagon tongue, ate venison and dumplings, using his bowie knife, and Big Betsy Cobb kept filling his plate until he was forced to say, "Enough. By grab, enough! Woman, you'll spile me for heaven giving me food like that."

She was flattered and deprecating. "Pshaw, nobody can cook really good on such a fire. You can make it wholesome and lasting, but nobody can cook fancy."

"This is fancy enough for me," John said with sincerity.

"Yes, but pies and cakes and things like that—such *mean* something to a woman. Oh, how happy I'll be to get in my new home over the mountain! I don't mind telling you I was suspicious that we'd ever *get* there with that Hames guiding us. It wasn't *him* so much. I wouldn't have been so suspicious of him. It was those men he brought along. You saw 'em—those gunmen."

"I saw 'em."

"Of course, I got nothing agin' guns, country being what it is. I carry this old horse pistol myself. Woman all alone, got to protect herself. By the way, Brother John, be you a married man?"

"No-o," said John warily.

"I buried my husband." Betsy blew her nose. "Back on the Platte, t'other side of Fort Laramie. Died of the horse croup. It was great shock to me. A dreadful shock." Then she brightened. "But the Reverend preached a beautiful sermon. All about the Land where we ne'er say good-by. A wonderful man, my Mr. Cobb, though he *did* take a little drop of likker now and again." She looked down on him. "Brother John, I *do* hope you're not a drinking man."

John got up as soon as he conveniently could, and hunted out the Parson.

"Danged widda woman," he said. "Got her cap perched for me. No use, o' course. When I settle down it's a Blackfoot gal for me."

"Don't find squaws turning out her brand of stew," said the Parson.

"True, but ye don't find a squaw that takes such a whopping big delight out o' burying her husband, neither." He got his cheek loaded with blackjack natural twist and stood looking at Hames's group of men, who were camped by the river. "*They* ain't farmers."

"Gold hunters, stringing along for the lift. We might be thankful for 'em. Fight Injuns. Palouse and Bannocks being what they are."

John recognized the type, frontier renegades, too lazy for work, and not nervy enough for banditry.

"Who be the long, tall, limber one with the chawed-off whiskers?"

"Calls himself Vogel."

"Sure, Vogel."

John remembered—Ed Vogel, Placerville. He had shot a man in the back there. A gambler named Sagrue. Sagrue had just stepped down from a platform sidewalk by Gorman's bakery, and there was Vogel with his Navy in the shadows. They'd have hanged him that night, but he took to the timber until the affair blew over. Later on, John had heard, Vogel joined the Bobtail Spruce gang, and then informed on them, turning them over to the vigilantes for a measly 18 ounces of gold. All that had been years ago, back in the 50's, and he had rather thought Vogel would be dead by this time, but he wasn't. He was alive, dirty and lousy as ever.

"Who's the others?"

"Short one's Little Tom. He's not so bad. Laughs and jokes all the time, but I'd guess he was on the run from *something*. Black one's Sanchez, he's a Mexican; then the big fellow with the ox-yoke mustache is Moose Petley, used to be a whisky trader among the Piutes; and that sort of fat one is Belly River Bob, he's drunk all the time."

"They're cooking up something for me, Parson, and I don't like it."

"Forget 'em. Joe Wood will keep these pilgrims in line. They complain, but they stick by him just the same. He swung this deal, you know. Bought the White Pine land from the old Western Fur Co. at bankruptcy court in St. Louis, bought 'er for a song, the finest land in all the Nor'west. Uncommonly smart man, Joe Wood. They'll meet, and they'll jaw, but they'll do what he says. And just between us, he's a mite suspicious of that Hames."

"How about his daughter?"

"Lela? Poor little dove! I tell you, John, it makes me choke up from sorrow thinking about her, trying to choose between Hames and that no-account banjo player, Rusty McCabe. She's seventeen, you know, and nigh onto being an old maid."

With supper finished, Joe Wood called the meeting as he had promised, and although Ambrose Stocker had his say, and a chinless, tall man named Wally Snite arose in opposition to taking John as guide, there was no serious threat to Wood's leadership.

In conclusion Wood said, "I don't expect any division of opinion about the route to the Bitterroot anyhow. Hames will have his say. We all will have our say. And if there's any doubt we'll vote on it."

That apparently satisfied everyone with the exception of Snite, and of Hames, who shrugged to indicate it meant nothing to him, anyway. Hames was a freight operator on his way to look over the possibilities of Montana territory, and his attachment to this wagon train was just a favor, or at least that was the impression he attempted to convey.

Hames, said John to himself. Yes, he had heard of a Pelton & Hames outfit down in Colorado. Unless he was mistaken it was Pelton & Hames who used to put sleeper guards inside a stagecoach they ran between Denver and French Bar—men disguised as miners or drummers, and a mighty low-down trick it was on road agents. Pelton & Hames, he heard, had gone broke, which served them right, and Hames being here fitted in with that.

However, right now it was Vogel rather than Hames who troubled him. Vogel would recognize him. Vogel might cause him trouble.

He ambled toward a little cut-bank fronted by spruce where Moose Petley, Sanchez, and Belly River Bob had built a fire and stretched some canvas against the wind that blew down cold from the mountain passes. No sign of Vogel.

Moose Petley and Belly River Bob were engaged in an argument, their voices raised, cursing each other. Their argument concerned the shape of the world, with Petley maintaining it was round and Bob that it was flat.

John said, walking into the light of the wind-whipped fire, "You're both wrong. If ye want to know what the world is, it's square."

"Well, that's the damnedest-fool thing I ever *did*

hear," said Moose Petley, giving him an ugly stare and looking to be sure where his Navy was.

John said, "In the Old Testament it says so. Thar it is in black and white. 'They come from the four corners of the world.' And who be you or me or any of us to argue with Scripture?"

Moose shouted, "I don't care if the Scripture says it or if the gov'ment says it, the world's round. There was a fellow sailed around it."

"Who was he?" asked Belly River Bob.

"I forget his name. He's dead now."

"You're damned right he's dead because if he sailed out there too far he'd fall over the edge and that'd pretty well be the end of *him*."

"Well, how about those fellows, Chiny traders, sail from San Francisco to Canton, and around Good Hope to London, and then over to Noo Yawk, and maybe around the Horn to Californy again? How do you figure that?"

Bob said, spitting and wiping his chin, "I got that figured out, too. Only one answer to it. The world *is* round in a way, but not round like a ball, but round like a saucer. It *has* to be, as anybody with common sense could see, because otherwise the oceans would all run out over the edge and it'd be dry land, dry as a bone. So these fellows that sail to Chiny just go out and get turned around somewhere."

They argued some more without Belly River Bob giving an inch in his contention until Petley in a rage drew his bowie and lunged forward with its needle-sharp point against Bob's stomach. "Shut up, damn you!" he bellowed. "Shut up or I'll whack your liver out. If they's one thing I cain't stand it's an ignorant man."

"All right," said Bob, "you win the argument."

They fell silent. Moose sat back, the bowie still drawn, and commenced picking his teeth.

"You make a specialty of guiding wagon trains?" he asked.

John nodded. "And you? You be a farmer?"

"I plant the soil."

"I'd hazard the guess that the things you boys plant won't sprout till Judgment Day."

"Say, that's pretty good!" Moose said, slapping his leg.

The Mexican, Sanchez, sat smiling to himself. Now he spoke. "Señor, I can see you are very sharp at guessing of a man his profession. Could you guess mine? I am a barber. If you at any time decide you need a shave—"

"You ain't going to get around *my* throat with no razor."

"Mine neither" muttered Belly River Bob.

Vogel was coming. John saw him, a long-armed, long-legged, double-jointed man, cutting over from Snite's wagon. He was dressed in homespuns. On his head was a hat so wide and floppy he had to fold back the brim and pin it to keep it from falling across his face. He carried two guns with the holsters fastened to his legs, their ends forward so the gun butts stuck back, threatening with each step to fall to the ground, but they never did.

"Well, good night to ye," John said to the boys by the fire, and walked out to meet Vogel.

"Hello, Ed," John said to him.

Vogel drew up at sound of the name. "My name ain't Ed, it's—"

"Well, good. So mine isn't Comanche John, either. In other words, I'm willing to forget about Californy if you are."

Vogel laughed then, showing a set of tobacco-browned teeth that looked black in the half-dark. "So that's it! You were afeared I'd talk."

"Not afeared. Just wanted to tell ye that if one of these mornings somebody called me 'Comanche John' I'd walk right over and shoot you on general principles."

"You don't need to worry about me." Vogel was tensely serious, staring John in the eyes. "I'll not turn informer on my own kind."

"How about the Bobtail Spruce gang?"

"That's a dirty lie. When the Californy stranglers weren't clever enough to get their ropes on me they spread that story hoping one of the old gang would kill me, but it's a lie."

But John knew it was not a lie. They talked for a while, and he bid Vogel good night. It was dark then, an early darkness with clouds in black layers on the horizon. He got his bedroll. The Parson found him and said, "You're welcome to pitch camp in my wagon," but John refused, saying he was "a creetur of the free and open," and carried his robes down to the river and along it and back into the brush. He knew that a man was following, so he waited.

"Here I be," said John.

The man was Hames. He walked up and, with perfect, cool civility, said, "How much have they offered you to guide them to White Pine?"

"Not a great deal. In fact, not even a cent."

Hames laughed. "Just being a good fellow!"

John decided to take it easy and not start a ruckus. "That ornery old Parson, he saved my hide one time. My *neck*, I should say. Accused of highway robbery. Of course, I was innocent as a babe unborn. But he saved me. Saved my neck and then he took enough interest in me to save my eternal soul from the fires of hell. Oh-h! What a hell that Parson did save me from! Described it to me. A fearful place. The wicked all tied down with hot coals all over their bare backs. Screaming and gnashing of teeth. I tell you, it would make a man examine his consicence. Hames, how long has it been since you examined your conscience?"

"My conscience serves me." He had taken some currency from a belt inside his antelope shirt. "There's two hundred dollars here," he said. "Enough to ride yonder and buy stage passage to Bannock."

John did not touch the money. "Greenbacks? Wuthless Union paper. Likely Robbie Lee has tooken Washington by this time. Getting mighty close last dispatch I seen. By now, that paper's not worth more'n ten cents on the dollar."

"All right, I'll give you gold."

He looked at him narrow-eyed. "You'd pay *gold* to git rid o' me? Why?"

Hames showed traces of his brittle temper once again. "What do you care as long as you're paid?"

John, leaning against a tree, rubbed back and forth to scratch his back while keeping his thumbs hooked in his twin gun belts. His right hand was still slightly lame from the breaking Hames had tried to give it.

"Well?" said Hames.

"Waal, no."

Hames, controlling a tight tremble in his voice, said, "I won't have you here."

"No-o?"

"No."

"You going to run me out?"

"Yes."

"Why?"

"I know who you are."

"You want to save 'em from me?"

"That's it."

"Well, you have taken a fancy to these people, you really have."

"I mean it. You get out or I'll make it hot for you."

"How long have I got?"

"Until tomorrow morning."

"Thank-ee," said John. "Thank-ee very much."

CHAPTER THREE

JOHN SLEPT deep in the brush—slept lightly with sounds awakening him half a dozen times during the night. It was still dark with stars out when somebody rang a bell, awakening the camp; it was time to get going.

He pulled on his boots; he had taken off nothing else. The night frost had placed a brittleness in the grass so it crunched underfoot. He saddled his horse, made a roll of his bed, and rode to camp.

The first wagons started out, gee-hawing and creaking through the cold. There was no communal fire this morning; from several wagon stovepipes smoke was coming and the occupants of these had warm breakfasts, but others ate cold dummy as they walked beside their teams, swinging their whips, fighting to get away first, to win a margin of distance against possible delay from breakdown, to get first chance at the grass, because making it over the pass or being left stranded along the way would depend on a man's stock, and a horse or mule pulled his weight or fell in the traces depending on the food he found along the way.

John found Big Betsy Cobb working like a man, backing a team of refractory bays up to the trees. She brushed off his offer to help. There was no smoke from her stovepipe, anyhow, no chance for hot breakfast there, so John walked on to help the Parson, who drove an old Conestoga held together by rawhide, pulled by a wiry four-horse team of Injun ponies.

"By grab," said John, "I wouldn't drive this outfit a mile for water. I'd pack-saddle over the hump and leave this wagon behind."

"She's rattly," said the Parson, "but she's tough. Don't let that rawhide fool you. Now you take two pieces of oak doweled and mortised together, give it a bend, and what happens? She breaks, especially in the dry climate. But rawhide *gives*. New wagon is too stiff. Give me an old one every time. This'n crawls over the rocks like a snake."

"Mind if I keep this here?" he asked, tossing his bed over the endgate. "Did ye hear about Hames telling me to clear out?"

"I was at the meeting."

"This war since the meeting. He offered me two hundred dollars. Think of that—two hundred dollars. Gold."

He let the Parson think about it and scouted ahead on a borrowed horse, giving the gunpowder a chance to graze. From a high pinnacle he saw the wagon train strung out along miles of valley. He rested, napped, and still he could see it, so slowly moving. To the east and north rose the Bitterroots already white with snow; in the west were the low rounded summits of the Salmon River Range, all misty autumn purple. In another day they would reach Salmon River and follow it briefly until it made its big swing to the west, when their trail would keep going north, up, up, and up to the ridge of the world, the main range of the Rockies, before dropping down on the Bitterroot River.

He saw Hames, but only from a distance. The day passed. Hames made no move to back up his threat. John again warily hid his bed. The country now broadened out, with small hills almost devoid of timber. The Lemhi joined the Salmon. There was grass aplenty here, grass that blew waves in the wind. He found Joe Wood talking to a young, very red-faced farmer named O'Donnell.

"If I was a farmer," John said, jogging the gunpowder into talking range, "damned if I wouldn't stop right here. I been up and down this country for many a year, and this Salmon beats 'em all."

"We already own our land," Wood said with a tight set to his lips. "We'll go on to the White Pine."

"So I figured." He nodded toward the grass. "You won't find much feed when the mountains commence, and that'll be damned sudden. Mighty long haul to the top, and mighty long on t'other side. I know there's blizzard in the air, but if this was my outfit I'd camp maybe two days, gamble that way, just to put some strength in the horses." He could tell that something was troubling Wood, so he said, "Out with it! Whatever ye got in your craw?"

"I've been told you're a bandit on the jump from the vigilantes over in the Montana."

John thought about it, squinting off while his jaw

revolved on his chaw of tobacco. "Mighty big, this country. Might-ee broad, and twice as wild. This be the wild Nor'west, and she's different than Missouri. Ye meet a man out on the trail, and ye don't ask who he was, or what he was. It's what he *is* that counts. Which bandit am I supposed to be, Whisky George or Zip Skinner, one o' them?"

"Comanche John."

"Yip-ee!" said John. "Why, that's top riffle. Why, *I'm* the most famous road agent of 'em all. *I'm* the one they wrote the song about!"

O'Donnell in his serious manner said to Wood, "I would rather be trusting *him*."

"Never mind," said Wood.

They decided to lay over one day for the grass, and to make wagon repairs before the tough climb began. All day John was aware of the talk being circulated against him, not only that he was Comanche John, but that he was in league with the remnants of the Snake River Gang, that the Snake River Gang might well be waiting in ambush to get their horses and supplies once they were on the Bitterroot side. By the time darkness came, the suspicion of the camp was something he could *feel*.

"They know who I be," he said to the Parson.

"O' course they know. And whose fault is it? You getting Rusty to sing that blame' song every chance you get!"

"I doubt that was it," and his eyes were on Hames's camp.

"Now, don't you start any trouble."

"I'll guarantee this—I'll start no more trouble than I can finish."

A while later, when Big Betsy Cobb was ladling stew into an iron plate for him, she said, "Brother John, there's a story about this camp that you're that ornery, no-account, killing, robbing Comanche John, and I want ye to know I'm taking no belief in it."

"Thank-ee," said John. "Only I hear he ain't so bad. Steals from the rich to give to the poor. Confines his killin' strictly to varmints, abolitionists, and that ilk."

He ate, wiped up the last bit of gravy on a biscuit, ate that, and dropped the plate back in the plunder box. Then he cut over through river brush to the spot where he'd left his bed.

Suddenly he was aware of danger—a slight movement, a sound, a danger he seemed to *smell*. What caused him to dip his head and dive forward he never knew, but he *did*, and powder flame burst in his face, and there was a wind-whip of lead passing, plucking at the crown of his black slouch hat.

He was face down in the clay dirt. He wanted to draw and shoot, but he fought back the urge. The ambusher was only a dozen steps away, across a little gully, on slightly higher ground, waiting for his slightest movement.

He was there a quarter or half a minute that seemed much longer. He could hear men talking, coming from camp, wondering what the shot was. Then he heard a crack of brush on the river side, and sensed that he was safe. Still cautious, drawing a Navy, he sat up and inspected the nick the bullet had put in his hat.

The shot caused no alarm. No one came to investigate. He prowled the brush. It was almost dark now, but across the gully, pressed in the soft clay ground, he saw the ambusher's tracks—moccasin tracks, the toed-in moccasin tracks that meant only one man—Vogel.

He moved his bed. Then he moved his horse, picketing the gunpowder for an easy getaway if one proved necessary. He inspected the loading of both Navies and put them back in their holsters, just so. That completed, he walked through the dark to the small fire where the renegades were broiling venison ribs and baking doughgod wrapped snail-like around sticks and propped over the coals. Hunkered, tending the cooking, were Belly River Bob and Moose Petley; Sanchez was a shadow and a shine of oily skin in the background; and in the middle of things, swaggering around on his double-jointed legs, was Vogel.

"You're damned right I kilt him," Vogel was braying, answering some doubt on the part of his hearers. "I was there, waiting for him, and when he came up and saw me, well!" He laughed and moved around, swinging his shoulders. "Well, you know how it is, a gunman builds a rep, gets to believing the stories they tell about him, but when he comes right face up against it he turns coward. So it was with Comanche John. Tried to git away along the ground, but I blasted the whole top of his head off."

"You tell Hames?" Petley asked.

"Naw. Not yet. Don't want to interfere with his love-makin'. That redheaded sprout was playing his banjo for her this afternoon, and she *liked* it. Hames will kill that kid just like I kilt the Comanche."

Sanchez was looking into the shadows, the firelight showing on his teeth as he grinned. "Eh, señor, do you believe in ghosts?"

"What?" said Vogel.

"Why, I thought I saw the ghost of your dead man."

John said, "Why, yes, here *I* be, and no ghost, either. Vogel, what was that you were saying, about a man turning coward when he runs face up against it?"

For a second Vogel's face was slack from shock and sick fear. Then he recovered and tried to bluster it out. "I warn't talking about *you*. I—"

"You got mighty poor style with those guns of yours," John said. "And you be a *Californy* man, too. I hate to see a Californy man git vulgar with guns—pride, ye know, being a Californy man myself. So I decided it was up to me to give ye a lesson. For instance, when ye draw, don't grip hard and jerk. Do it slow. Take your time. Make your arm sort of loose, then lift. Just lift that loose arm with your shoulder. I tell ye what, Vogel, let's both of us draw and I'll show ye what your mistake is."

"No."

"Go ahead. Draw your gun."

"No." Vogel wanted to get away, but he was in the open and there was no cover for twenty feet. He took a step back, shaking his head hard. "I'm not going to draw. You'd kill me if I drew. You're trying to git me to draw and kill me. But you don't dare kill me if I don't draw. They'll hang you. They will sure if you kill me."

"Now *that's* something else. Lack of confidence. That's pizen to a gunman. Well, if you won't draw first, I'll have to draw for ye. Watch my right hand, now. See how I do it. Up, like this!"

He drew the right-hand Navy, but the hammer caught in the bottom of his jacket, and that pulled it free of his hand. The gun fell. He made a grab for it and hit it instead, knocking it five or six feet away from him. He started for it, apparently off guard, and Vogel, thinking he saw his chance, jumped back and drew both guns.

They were out of the leather but John, straightening with a half-slouched pivot, had his left-hand Navy. He hesitated for a fragment of time. He gave the illusion of taking his sweet time while Vogel jerked his guns fast as a coiling snake.

The Navy exploded with a pencil of flame, spinning Vogel so one of his long legs seemed to wrap around the other. Vogel lunged, with both guns exploding at his own boot toes. He went down with his hat tumbling off and his face on top of the hat. And he lay there with the life knocked out of him.

John watched him. He watched and kept sight of the others and blew smoke from the muzzle of his Navy. He located the other gun, picked it up, and reholstered it. For those shocked seconds nobody had spoken a word. Then he drawled, "Thar, see what I mean? He *jerked*. He wasn't loose and relaxed like he should have been. Muscles were too tight."

"You have killed him, señor!" Sanchez burst out.

"Why, yes, I believe I have. But it's nothing to be proud of. I been running into a pretty poor breed of gunmen lately."

CHAPTER FOUR

HE WANDERED OFF into the bushes. He was well hidden in the river trees when news of the shooting reached camp. He hunkered, and chawed, and listened. He could hear the indignant voice of Ambrose Stocker braying, "He ought to be hung. I say he's a killer and he ought to be hung!"

They held a meeting at Joe Wood's wagon. Stocker was still shouting at the top of his voice. Others had started to shout, too—some of them on Stocker's side, and some saying he should shut up and give *them* a chance to speak. Wood, a quiet man, could get nowhere. Finally Hames, with the advantage of height and a voice that was as good as Stocker's, took command and made a speech.

Why, naturally there was only one course to follow, he said. California had found that out, so had Colorado, and so had they down on the Snake River. So had they, if the news was true, over on the Beaverhead. They had used rope. There was only one thing to do with killers of John's cut and that was to hang them.

A wagoner named Kippen said, "*Hang* him? Let's catch him first."

"Yes," shouted Stocker, "let's not wait any longer. Let's go fetch him."

"He's run for it." Kippen was disgusted. "That's the trouble with you. You spend all your strength talking."

"Well, why didn't *you* chase him?"

"I haven't lost any road agents," said Kippen.

"Why, that's coward talk. That's what it is, it's cowardly."

"I'm not afraid of you, Stocker."

"We won't fight among ourselves!" Joe Wood had finally made himself heard. "It isn't that important."

"A man has been killed," cried Hames; "isn't that important?"

O'Donnell then tried to make a speech. He pointed out that Vogel had bragged every day what a killer he was. This infuriated Hames, who started to shout him down, but O'Donnell had friends who insisted that he have his say.

"He carried two guns," said O'Donnell. "He had notches cut in the handles. Yes, notches. He was *proud* of his killing. Every day he swaggered and talked of his killing. I say, let the killers kill each other. We should have no part in it."

The argument was by no means over, but the two sides were quite evenly divided, and it has to be strongly against a man before there's hanging, so John felt safe enough to come around by the Parson's wagon for a better look-see.

"You got blood on your hands!" the Widow Cobb said low in her throat, glimpsing him. "I don't know but what I'm shocked and grieved at you, Brother John. You killed a human being and you'll answer for it at Judgment."

"So'd young David have blood on his hands when he knocked down Goliath, but that didn't prevent him singing his psalms. Behold, woman, I carry my Navies to draw on the side o' righteousness and that's more'n I can say for *some* of the *unregenerated* varmints around here."

"Glory be, you may have some wisdom there. I don't cotton to gun fight, but if it had to be, I'd rather it'd be that dirty, no-account, swaggering, cursing Ed Vogel than 'most anybody I know. Well, be that as it may, we got to give him a Christian burial. We got to lay him out and comb him, and I wouldn't be surprised if we had to de-louse him."

"Lice don't stick with a dead man, Sister Betsy," said a small, tired-looking woman, Ambrose Stocker's wife. "That's a tried and true test for the dead. My mother's people were much afflicted with the rigid fits, and

Grandmother Toston always tried 'em with a louse, and if the louse crawled off they were dead. They're the lower creeturs, and they got a seventh instinct not known to man."

"When I'm rigid," said John, "you don't need to bother with the louse, you can just bury me."

"Oh," said the Widow Cobb, "why *couldn't* this have happened *yesterday* instead of tonight? Now everybody will be wanting to roll before sunup and the Reverend will have little if any chance for his sermon. Well, nothing can be done about it, I suppose. We'll just *have* to make out. It must needs be a nighttime service. They can be very nice. Very nice. I do wish we had plumes. They add *such* a touch. I wish the Reverend would come over here and tell us if he intends to preach brimstone."

"That's what I like," said John, "brimstone."

A third woman, Mrs. O'Donnell, said, "I don't care much for brimstone at a funeral. I think you ought to go easy on the dead, especially if there's relatives present."

John said, "I guess I was closer to Vogel than anybody else, knew him since '49, both come from Pike County. Everybody from Pike County, Missouri, is related to everybody else. So, being sort of a relative, I give my consent."

They had caught sight of John, and there came Phelps and Stocker with a horse pistol and a shotgun respectively. John was now slightly apprehensive, for he had no desire to be forced into trading shots with the emigrants.

"Put the guns down, boys," he said, ambling toward them, tired and dragging his jackboots. "I got no fight with you. I kilt a man, true. Kilt him in a gun duel. Self-defense. Why, they wouldn't even jail me for that in Illini."

Stocker shouted, "You went over there on the prod, looking for him. You shot him down in cold blood."

"Who said?"

"Moose Petley, Belly Rover Bob, all of 'em."

"Oh, *them*." He wanted to retreat but those guns were on him. *Many* of the emigrants were fingering guns. He said, "Something else, something I didn't tell ye. He tried to ambush me. Yonder, by the river, around twilight. That was the shot ye all heared. I dove and it saved me. Thought he'd kilt me, he did."

Stocker laughed and said, "Oh, hell!"

There was other talk, low talk; nobody believed him. Wood was looking around, troubled, getting ready to mount the steps. Wood was a great one for democracy; he would put it to an open vote and that might be bad.

John started looking around for retreat when Rusty McCabe, with a frightened expression, climbed to the steps and said shakily, "Hold on, I saw it." Rusty did not look at Hames. He was scared of Hames, but he was talking anyway. His face looked white as a toadstool in the light, his freckles standing out. It was cold, but there was a shine of perspiration above his eyebrows. He went on: "We—I—I was over hunting for Lafe's gray mare, saw it all. Saw Vogel try to ambush him. Thought he was dead—*John* was dead. Didn't know what to do. I came over here. I guess I was scared. I thought Vogel would kill me."

Hames shouted, "That's a plain lie. Look how they pal up together, him and John, him always singing that song."

Wood said in his quiet voice that carried so well, "Rusty! Somebody was with you!"

Rusty was unable to say no. He was looking across the heads of the crowd, and a second later, also frightened and sick, 13-year-old Veltis Stott crept into view. "Yah. I saw it, yah." He nodded his head very hard. In fright, with his long blond hair hanging over his face and his eyes shining through it, he looked idiotic. But he was telling the truth. No one could doubt he was telling the truth.

Wood said, "You have nothing to be afraid of. Was it like he said?"

"Yah."

Hames said, "you believe *them!*" He tossed his head with a bitter laugh. He took off his beaver hat and rubbed his palm across his forehead. "Look at what you're believing—*them!*" And turning in contempt he went long-striding toward his wagon.

CHAPTER FIVE

AS FOR THE FUNERAL, Big Betsy's worst fears were realized. The wagoners, already kept up late, were impatient for their beds and fewer than half of them came to the service. There was no coffin, of course, and no funeral really *looks* like a funeral without one. To make it worse, the Parson was not up to his usual form, only drawing a few morals on the fate of the unregenerated, and not even touching on the weeping and the gnashing and the seven seas of sulphurous fire.

"Well, maybe it's for the best," Betsy said. "I know it might sound peculiar to some, but I *am* relieved my husband, my sainted Mr. Cobb, passed away on the Platte where things weren't hurried, and we could take a decent time to bury him. It's my notion that there's nothing throws a crimp into a funeral like an overhurried preacher."

It turned colder in the night with a few crystals of snow. In the darkness of early morning, when the wagon train got into movement, the snow had stopped, but clouds remained, hovering over the mountains a misty gray. The wagons pulled harder in the cold, the bumps of the rocky trail seemed worse. They camped again on the Salmon, in thicker timber, with the mountains rising steeply from the narrow valley.

Next day the main stream was left behind, and they followed the North Fork. The road became narrow. Originally it was an Indian trail, later used by fur traders who found they could cross with two-wheeled

carts, and next, with wagons, by the Mormon party in
'52, and by the Deer Valley settlers under Brighton
three years later. Now, however, everyone seemed
bound for the gold camps of Bannock and Hangtown,
and took the Bannock Pass far to the south; or they
came from the Snake River diggings, following the
Lolo to Hell Gate, so now the road was poorly traveled. Windfalls continually blocked the way and had
to be chopped out. There were slides and fallen boulders. In places the road was little better than a pack-
horse trail with the mountain on one side and the
swift waters of the North Fork on the other, and wagons tilted so precariously that men had to hang to
their uphill sides to weight them against capsizing.

There was no cluster of wagons at night; they
camped in groups along the trail. A wind blew down
the deep valley with a feel of winter that made men
turn their backs, and eat in the shelter of canvas, or
inside their wagons.

"What the hell kind of a country you takin' us to?"
Phelps said to Comanche John. "Winter come in Sep-
tember?"

"*This* is my calendar." John meant his knees and
hips, which became slightly lame after riding in the
cold. "These mountain passes snow up early; but lower down, at White Pine where ye be headed, I'd wager
on some fine weather yet."

"But how long to *get* there? Oh, *you* don't need to
fret, all you have to do is tepee in with the Injuns, I
suppose, but *we* got to build some sort of shelter
against the cold. What route you plan to guide us to
the White Pine?"

"Only *good* way there is—up to Hell Gate, then
easy following the freight road on the Clark's, and
then south again."

"North, and east, and back again. What kind of
judgment is that? Why not cut across?"

"Maybe ye can fly across like an eagle?"

"There's a cut-across road by Big Hole Pass. How
about that?"

"You been talking to Hames, ain't ye? Oh, I know he's been boosting the Big Hole, trying to say my route is the long way around. It's long, all right, but it will *git* you thar."

He could see that Phelps didn't believe him. Phelps, Stocker, and Snite were strong for Hames, and it would be a fine ruckus trying to hold the train together once they reached the Big Hole turnoff.

John walked to the Parson's wagon. The old man was shivering, trying to start a fire with damp wood in his little Santa Fe stove. A tallow dip, a bit of wool lying in a can of half-congealed bear grease, gave the crowded, tunnel-like interior of the wagon a flickering, ruddy glow.

"We be headed for trouble at the Big Hole turnoff," John said. "I'll bet that rangy woolly-wolf has talked half the wagons into turning east."

"Hames? He ain't convinced Wood. Nor Lela, because she'll stick with her pa. And where Lela goes, Hames will go. He's enamored o' her."

"But you sure Wood will stick fast to going by Hell Gate?"

"He'll go. Don't you worry about Wood. He's got an uncommon level head for a Pikes Peaker."

The Parson was suffering from rheumatics, so John stayed with him and helped with his work. He slept in the wagon. He was awakened before dawn. Already wagons were moving, wagons wanted to get past. He hitched and drove while the Parson cooked breakfast. The trail steepened. Tandem wagons had to be disconnected and pulled one at a time. Each time this happened, all the following wagons were delayed. Snow commenced to appear. The clouds that for three days had hung low, hiding the mountaintops, rose to reveal a new land, a land of towering peaks and ridges, a wilderness of rock already deep in snow. The mountains extended range after range, apparently forever making more than one of the wagoners feel his own insignificance, placing a cold knot in his middle, this plunging into a wintery, inhospitable land.

At a meeting that night Hames produced a map cut from a St. Louis paper some years before, and now ready to fall apart at the folds from long carrying. It showed no route at all to the Bitterroot, but two-thirds to the crest they were struggling toward was a heavy, double line pointing east marked: *Big Hole Pass.* The double line ran on, straight to Deer Lodge Valley, and at the bottom was the legend: *Good Wagon Road.*

"Now *he* would be a guide for us," said John. "The editor of that St. Looey paper. Look down here. He's got his road going up the wrong side of the Salmon."

His observation served to discredit the map, but still there was strong sentiment for taking Hames's advice and turning toward the Big Hole.

Later, inside the Parson's wagon, John said, "Well, let 'em! Let 'em take their chicken crates and run 'em over the brink of hell if that's their choice. I'll ride by myself and shift for myself."

"No, John, you won't. You won't because I made a Christian of you, and when you're a Christian you have responsibilities. It's not all wine and white bread when you're a Christian. Part of it is sackcloth and ashes, and I promised to guide 'em to Fort Hall myself, and I did. And I promised I'd provide a dependable guide to the White Pine, and that dependable guide is *you*. Now have a cup of tea whilst I finish the biscuit. It'll put new fight into you."

John ate. By grab, if there was one thing he didn't need it was any more fight. He had plenty of fight. He left to have a word with Joe Wood. It was dark, the clouds were down again, and there was a stiff, cold wind. He walked up the grade, past huddled wagons, his hands inside his jacket and his hat down against wind. There was Joe Wood's wagon, a light brightening its canvas top, and shadows moving around. It was about as full of men as it could be. They were holding a meeting—another powwow.

"T' hell with 'em!" he muttered.

Wagons filled the trail, leaving scant room for a man to walk without climbing rocks and timber. Snow had settled in, ankle-deep in places, and he could feel it strike cold through a rent in the instep of his right boot.

"I'm in damn poor shape for winter," he muttered. "No boots, no grubstake, no fat on my horse and none on me, neither. By grab, this is my last winter of this. I'm about sick of being a Christian. I'm going to find me a Blackfoot gal, snug tepee, somebody to look out for my comfort. Plenty buffalo jerky, plenty camas roots, plenty dried chokecherry. Worse things in the world than buffalo, camas, and chokecherry."

He was still muttering, getting his jacket tied against the cold, when he noticed the two saddle horses tied on the lee side of Wally Snite's wagon. One of them was the big, bald-faced sorrel that Moose Pet-ley liked to ride, and though it was too dark to be sure, he thought the other belonged to Little Tom. They were gone most of the time, those two, leaving Belly River Bob and the Mexican to drive the big, al-most empty Pittsburgh wagon and herd the dozen head of saddle stock that formed Hames's outfit—the outfit he intended going into the freight business with when he got to the Montana side.

He kept talking to himself because talking seemed to help keep him warm. "Scouting for Injuns. *Their* story. Makin' *friends* with the Injuns, more like. And that outfit. *Freight* business. Need plenty wagons, plenty stock for the freight business. Yes, he would. And where would he get 'em? Just where? Why, here."

That last was a bad thought. But it would be like taking rabbit away from a catamount, taking horse-and-wagon outfits away from these farmers. Sanchez, Petley, Belly River, and Little Tom might be good fighting men, but they weren't *that* good. And Ed Vo-gel wasn't around any more, so that left Hames a man short. No, they wouldn't try it. Not without a lot of help, and John couldn't see where he would find help.

He stopped suddenly. Someone was there, con-cealed in the shadow of a supply wagon. A man and a girl. They stood very still, and it took him a second to realize that the girl was Lela Wood and the man Rusty McCabe.

John put them at ease by saying, "Just been up tucking that danged old preacher in bed. Pining away, he is. Just too many funerals and not enough weddings. Turning morbid. Nothing *I* could do about it short of marrying that Widda Cobb, and it wouldn't be the same as marrying young folks."

"Oh!" said Lela, acting as though she wanted to stop him, but of course really she *didn't;* gals always acted that way.

He pretended to have an interest in the camp and looked all around. Then he sidled close to Rusty and said from the side of his mouth, "Go head and ask her. See what she says."

After a tongue-tied moment Rusty said, "Lela—" and bogged down.

"Oh, Rusty!" she said, on the verge of tears, and a moment later she had her head on his shoulder.

John plodded on, saying, "I just go along, doing good deeds b'side the way, gittin' business for the Parson."

He tended the gunpowder, finding a parklike area a quarter mile from camp where the grass was still untouched. He picketed the pony and, using his hat, rubbed all over his coat, thinking just a little extra attention paid off, keeping an animal in shape so he'd be able to make the long travel some day and save a man's life.

He went back to the road, to Joe Wood's wagon. Men were outside now, talking. The powwow had broken up. He stood quietly in the darkness listening to men as they passed. O'Donnell came along alone and John stopped him.

"Ho-up!" he said softly. "What's the excitement?"

"The men just got back from Big Hole Pass."

"What men?"

"Moose and Little Tom."

"I suppose they found pavement like in St. Loo?"

"There's been a gold strike."

"Whar?"

"They called it the Proctor Diggings."

"Oh, *that*."

"You've heard of it?"

"Fact is, I was to the Proctor not two month ago. Narrow gulches, five or six of 'em, in among the timber. Pay streak generally couple o' feet wide."

"It's no good?"

"What difference how good if all the ground is gone?"

"Why, yes. Only they said—"

"Oh, maybe some hardrock left. I saw three Chinymen making wages pounding up quartz in hand mortars. *Chinee* wages, but nothing to interest an American. You mean *that's* the big news?"

"I'll tell them what you said."

He hurried away, calling to the others, and there was another powwow in the dark.

"Where is that John? Where is he?" Ambrose Stocker came poking around the wagons.

"Here I be," said John.

"Oh."

He could not make out Stocker's face, only his big form, but he could guess the man's truculent expression.

"I don't think you been at the Proctor Diggings at all," said Stocker.

"Your priv'lege," said John.

"I think you're set on keeping us on this side of the mountains. *Why?* That's what I want to know. Just why?"

"It ain't because I enjoy your company."

"Just how you greasing *your* skillet in this? You think maybe you can cut a bigger slice of the gravel for yourself?"

"Now, Stocker, I've tooken all I'm going to." John meant it. His voice was quiet, but it *showed* that he meant it.

Stocker fell back a step. "I got friends here. I'm not

afeared of you or your guns. You won't get away with gunning me like you did Vogel."

"Now, Stocker. Don't you say too much. Stocker, let me advise you. I been up and down this country for a year or three and I been much amazed at how little trouble a man gits himself into by keeping a good lead string on his tongue."

"Well, all right, but I'll leave it to Lafe and to Dilworth if I didn't say that you'd try to blow cold air on it the first chance you got."

"Why didn't Petley and Little Tom stay at Proctor if it was so good?"

"They *staked* their gravel."

"And came back after you?"

"Yes."

"Then you aim to give up the White Pine and go to mining?"

A crowd had gathered around—men, women, and kids. It was for the women he intended his words about White Pine, but he soon learned that they were even more hungry for sudden wealth than their menfolk.

Mrs. Dilworth, who dressed in men's clothes and did the work of a man, said, "If I thought there was a chance for money *I'd* give up White Pine. I'd give it up in a minute." She thrust out her hands, palms up. "Look at 'em. Calluses like a man's. No colored mammy ever worked harder than *me* from slavery. Look at them hands; sometimes I think I ought to have 'em half-soled like you would a pair of boots. Born in a shanty not fit for a hawg. No floor, rain came through, married when I was thirteen years old. Oh, my men tried hard enough—both of 'em. Lord knows *I* tried hard enough. Slave all year for the locusts and green worms to eat up. Borry money and have the bank foreclose. Move to Kansas, scrimp and save and build three years on a house and just when you got a roof over your head, and a floor instead of the dirt, then the slavery people burn you out, *your own peo-*

ple. Look at that shoe." She thrust her foot out, waist high. "Home-tanned leather soled with green buffalo back. A slave in the cotton field don't wear nothing like that. No stockings, even. And what's at White Pine but more of the same? So if we got a chance for the gold, a chance to *git* and *have* and be able to buy a few of the better things, I say *let's take that chance.* Let's head for the Proctor."

The speech took John down a peg. "I'm sorry, ma'am." He really was. "I thought you folks loved the soil."

"We do. We love the soil, but I for one would like to have a little something so's I could work it like a human being and live like a human being instead of digging it and holing up in it like a badger. What I'd like to do is get a little stake of gold dust—not much, just a little, five or six hundred dollars even—and *then* go on to White Pine."

"It's up to you. If you want farm land, that's fine. If you want a whack at the gold first, that's fine, too. But if you *do* look for gold, be sensible, turn your wagons around, roll back to the Bannock Pass, to Beaverhead, Alder, to that country north of the Three Forks. That's the country for gold, and for silver, too, if you're willing to drill and hammer. But I think it's for you to decide which you're going to be, miners or farmers. By dang, I never seen a body that could be both at the same time."

Wally Snite, hiding in the background, jeered. "And by morning we'll be fighting over a pass that never was, and *he'll* be gone to grab the best of the Proctor Diggings for himself."

John chose to ignore him as he would ignore a barking terrier. "Tell ye what—it's still a pull to Big Hole turn-off. Why not send a couple of your own men over to look at the Proctor for themselves?"

Snite and a couple of the others were willing to jeer at that, too, but it appealed to the better heads among them, and at that moment Joe Wood came up. Informing himself of the dispute, he said, "Very well, let's have a couple of volunteers."

The only one anxious to go was Snite, but the others were unwilling to trust him, so the decision was put off until morning.

John returned to the Parson's wagon. He had just taken his boots off and started to unwrap the wool strips he used in place of regular socks when Mrs. Dilworth suddenly appeared at the back door and said, "Say, Wood has been looking all over for you."

John put his boots back on and once again walked up the road, past the wagons, now mostly quiet with folks gone to bed. At Joe Wood's a candle still burned, and he could see the shadow of someone moving around. He rapped. Wood said, "Come in," and John opened the endgate and climbed through.

"What were ye wanting?" John asked.

Wood had taken off his heavy wool jacket and was apparently getting ready for bed. Lela was not there.

"I didn't want anything," he said.

"Mrs. Dilworth said ye wanted to see me."

"How'd that fool woman get anything like that in her head?"

"Oh, the gold fever—it makes 'em imagine things." He laughed it off. "Anyhow, now I'm here, maybe we should talk a little. About the gold—it might be better than farming, after all."

"There isn't a man among us who knows the first thing about mining."

"No-o, but on the other hand it's been my observation that most folks are happier starving to death digging for gold than getting medium fat on a farm. With a farm you *know* you won't get far, but a mine is different. Never a miner that didn't have a million dollars just two feet ahead of his shovel."

"Yes, I suppose." Wood looked very tired. He was not a rugged man. "You've had a pretty rough time with these men. I understand. I suppose I understand better than anyone else. But once we get to the other side, once the road eases out, you'll find they're not un-reasonable."

"Provided we *git* to the other side. *Won't* if they vote for the Big Hole. Listen, I've been up thar. Not from here, but from yonder, traveling this way. Any-how, I had a look at her as far as the crest. Maybe you *could* get a wagon over. But it's a cliff route, a switch-back route. If there's deep snow, or if there's been a rock slide—"

"*They* were across it."

"Petley and Little Tom?" In his disgust, John was tempted to spit tobacco juice on the floor.

"You don't trust them?"

"Do you? They're renegades, back shooters, the worst. Why ain't they at the gold camps? I'll tell ye why—because even Bannock and Hangtown can't stomach 'em. They'd starch a rope down there, you take my word for it."

Joe Wood moved around, scratching his body through his knit woolen undershirt and looking John in the eyes. "What do you think of Hames?"

"You know what I think of him. Why did ye let him jine up?"

He raised his voice defensively. "He had a good rep-utation in Denver City. He was a freight operator. The war broke him, but he was a legitimate operator."

Yes, thought John, *the kind of legitimate operator that put sleeper guards inside his stagecoach, which was a low, unsporting trick on a road agent*. John was all for a coach owner protecting himself, but he should do it in the open, with guards that looked like guards, and not men done up in women's clothes, or in hard hats like patent-medicine drummers. Besides, he had heard it rumored that Hames had killed his partner, old W. J. "Rawhide" Pelton.

John said, "Now why would a big freight operator want to take to guiding wagon trains?"

"I told you, he went broke. He's headed north for a fresh start. The train gave him and his outfit protec-tion through the Indian country. This is bad country with those renegades from the Cayuse war pushed south. Them and the Bannocks. And how did we know you'd ever show up? We expected you at Fort Hall."

"You know what I think Hames has on his mind? I think he has a mind to strand ye in snow, get ye to pack over to Proctor; then *there* is his new freight outfit waiting for him—*your* horses and wagons."

"No!" cried Wood with such force John thought perhaps he had thought the same thing himself. "No, you're wrong about that!"

"It war done before, yonder in Oregon, wagon train coming across the Malheur attacked by Injuns, only they *warn't* Injuns, but white men in brown ocher and feathers, with a help from some *guides* with the train. I tell ye, there's no crime too low or devilish but a white man ain't tried it *some* time since the gold rush, and I say that's quite a record in just fourteen short—"

"Listen!" said Wood.

They stopped talking. There was something—not a sound, more like a tremble of the wagon. John instinctively moved into the shadows with hands dangling below the butts of his Navies. Something rustled a bit of loose canvas against the wagonbox. "Wind," said John.

"Yes. I thought it was somebody climbing around." He dismissed it from his mind and turned as if to reach something on the table, and at that instant the air was rocked by flame and explosion.

The gunshot had burst from only a few feet away—from the drawstring window at the forepart of the wagon.

John instinctively drew and spun. He fired both pistols, aiming below the window, hoping for a lucky shot when the man tried to escape.

Wood had been knocked across the table. He hung, bent over at the abdomen, his arms dangling. He slipped and fell, taking the candle with him. It was dark.

John dropped to one knee and felt for his pulse.

And now voices were coming that way, voices of men apparently on every side rushing closer.

One was Wally Snite: "It's Wood! That dirty killer Comanche John was in there with him! They were quarreling about sending men to Proctor. I think he killed him."

"Who?"

"Wood. He killed him. We should have hung him. I *said* we should have hung him."

John knew there was no time to waste. He slid backward boots first and dropped to the ground through the endgate door.

Men were bearing down on him through darkness from up and down the road. He crawled beneath the wagon. There, with one Navy drawn, he took a few seconds to estimate his chances.

On one side the bank dropped off across rocks the size of gravestones to the swift water of the North Fork. On the other, toward the mountainside where his horse waited, was a shoulder of ground, very steep-faced, almost bare at the crest.

Men were coming. Suddenly they were very close. They were all around the wagon. He could see the lower parts of their bodies, shadows, as they stopped, none of them wanting to be first inside the wagon.

Hames, from forty or fifty yards, called, "Is he in there?"

Dilworth answered, "We don't know."

"Well, go in after him."

"Dammit, I don't want to run into a pistol slug."

Lela was saying, "Where's my dad? How about my dad?" and John wanted to go out and comfort her, but of course he didn't.

At last somebody found the nerve to enter the wagon. John could feel his weight as he groped around, making the wagon shake on its springs. John had crawled forward; he was between the front wheels, he emerged on the hill side of the road. Men were all around, but darkness saved him. He walked. Someone spoke to him. "Lafe?" He grunted an answer. His voice went unrecognized. He kept walking. He speeded his step. Suddenly a man loomed ahead of him. A man running. They collided. The man's weight sent John staggering backward. It was Stocker. He sensed that Stocker was going for his gun, but John's right-hand Navy was already drawn.

"Covered!"

Stocker froze with a little gasp of breath.

John went on, very quietly: "Lift your gun. Two fingers. Thar. Now, drop it. Don't talk. Don't say a word. Just do as I tell ye and you'll end up being alive. Turn around. Head uphill. Walk."

At gunpoint he walked Stocker up the mountain, through timber, to the little open area where the gunpowder waited. Then he rested on his heels and instructed Stocker in putting the saddle on. It took about five minutes, and all the while, expecting to die at his first false move, Stocker said not a word.

"That's fine," said John. "Ye did a good job. Now stand back." He mounted, and at last put the Navy away. "Fare thee well." His grin was lost in the darkness. "Ye can go now. Ye can brag to your children and your children's children how ye once looked into the Navy of the one and gen-u-wine Comanche John and lived to tell the tale!"

CHAPTER SIX

COMANCHE JOHN rode through timber, following a dim deer track along the mountainside, taking his time, letting the pony pick his way, bending the pine branches aside, singing in a soft monotone, a new stanza of the song he had learned from Rusty:

> *"Thar's a forty-dozen highwaymen*
> *'Twixt Denver and the sea,*
> *But I sing of old Comanche John*
> *The toughest one thar be;*
> *He robbed the bank, he robbed the stage,*
> *He robbed the Yuba mail,*
> *And he left his private graveyards*
> *All along the Bannock trail.*

"By grab," he said "that's a fine verse. A bee-utiful verse. I'd like to find the mule skinner that wrote that verse and banquet him with likker."

He rode, hunting the rocky going to hide his trail in case of pursuit. Finally, satisfied with his precaution, he camped, building a tiny brush lean-to, sleeping rolled in his robe until the cold awakened him. He was tempted to ride on to Montana, but he delayed, thinking that after all the Parson, the Widow Cobb, and some of the others had put their faith in him. At midday, from a pinnacle, he caught sight of the wagon train. He watched it, slow-creeping, until dark, when camp was made at the Big Hole turnoff.

Here it was, then, the road Hames wanted them to take. It was up to them now to make up their minds. It would be rough on the Parson, now, trying to oppose him.

John shot a grouse, roasted it on a tiny fire, and ate it half raw with a chaw of tobacco for dessert. He slept, arising at hour intervals to stamp cold out of his body, and rode down cautiously to see what decision the emigrants had reached.

No decision at all, he decided. They had camped, had wagons torn down for repairs, stock out to graze to get a little reserve for the tough miles ahead. Apparently on a private mission, Moose Petley and Little Tom set off toward the east. He decided to follow them.

He kept them in sight for an hour; after that he trailed through the light snow. Toward evening two other horses joined them. A peculiar something about the new set of prints made him dismount for a closer inspection. These horses were unshod, but their hoofs had been covered by rawhide stockings, heat-shrunk to such hardness that even the mountain snow and damp did not loosen them. Indian horses, Palouse or Bannock.

He trailed through twilight and early darkness. A bleak ridge of solid stone rose on one side, and the cliff walls of a gulch lay on the other. He reached the crest of the range with the Big Hole country dropping away before him. There his nostrils, sharpened in the autumn freshness, detected the odor of wood smoke. It guided him to the brink of a little cirquelike valley containing a lake and meadow, an L-shaped log house, some corrals, and a horse shed.

He was surprised to find such a place so deep in the wilderness until he realized it was Desette's Rendezvous, where in the old days of the beaver trade a representative of the S. L. & Y. Company came each year to trade with Indians crossing over from Salmon River.

He did not go down immediately. He turned back, and at a distance of a mile, by a trickle of gulch water, found grass, and picketed his horse. Then he walked through timber, coming up to the house from the corral side.

A grease-dip light was burning in the closed end of a shed. He peeped through a hole in the chinking and saw five men, all of them half-breeds or Indians, cross-legged or sprawled on the earthen floor, playing a knife-and-stick game for gold coins. He had seen none of them before. He walked quietly around the shed, crossed an open area at the back of the house. Inside he could hear the dull mutter of voices, but no word was audible. Wary for a sentry, he circled and walked along the front, beneath a pole awning, past a parchment-covered window, to the door.

The door was closed, but it was whipsawed lumber, warped and ill fitting, so he could see inside. There, back to a fireplace, stood Moose Petley. A gaunt old Indian with hair cropped like a white man sat cross-legged before him. Two other men, Indians or breeds, were near by, and there were more, how many he did not know.

A soft whisper of footsteps told him of someone's approach from the direction of the horse shed. He looked for concealment. There was none handy, but the porch roof was supported by substantial timbers, the lower braces running solidly from pillars to the house. He reached, chinned himself up and over one of them, and crouched on one knee with head and back bent against the roofing as the man came in sight and walked directly beneath him, so close John could have dropped a foot and touched him.

He was a short, very broad man, and no Indian about him, just plain renegade. He went inside.

John stayed where he was. It was a fine place from which to listen and watch. He made himself comfortable by turning and lying full length. The timber was a scant six inches wide, but it had been squared, leaving its top side smooth and flat. With his hat rolled up to cushion the side of his head, he waited.

Their voices became audible. He could not hear most of what they said, but he could hear enough—they were planning an attack two days hence, three at most.

There was protracted wrangling. Many points remained to be settled. He stayed where he was, wishing to learn all that he could. He was cold. His feet had gone dead. He wanted to move, but a couple of Indians had come outside and were standing right beneath him. At last, after what seemed to be hours, the meeting broke up. Moose Petley, Little Tom, and the scarfaced Indian went toward the corral. Five or six minutes later he heard horses leaving. Then the scarfaced one came back alone.

"Good!" he said. "Big skookum, eh? Damn right. Plenty gold, plenty gun. Saddle horse. Work horse big *tyee*, saddle horse Injun. Plenty grub, too."

And they moved away, jabbering among themselves, mostly in an Indian dialect John did not understand, but no matter, he had heard enough. Now he knew how Hames planned to get hold of the wagon train—work stock and wagons for himself, saddle horses and guns for the Indians.

They were all gone now. It was his chance. He had to move now, before dawn trapped him there.

He felt for his guns. He raised himself and swung his legs over, held the beam with one hand, and lowered himself. He dropped, and his legs collapsed under him. He fell headlong. He tried to get up. He could not. His legs seemed to be paralyzed. An Indian shouted and ran toward him. He was on his knees. He could get no farther. And now there were more Indians, Indians from every direction, all around him. He had no chance to escape, even with the guns. He had to bluff it out.

He asked, "Whar's Moose? Little Tom?"

They did not seem to understand him. At last he managed to get to his feet. He stood with one hand braced against the logs.

"I'm a bit stiff," he said. "Long riding. Hames sent me. Big *tyee*, you savvy? Whar did ye say Petley was?"

One of the half-breeds pointed out across the mountains. He was explaining that Petley and Little Tom had left only minutes ago. Then the scarfaced one—a one-eyed old warrior with his left cheek deeply cleft from an old tomahawk wound—cried, "You come from wagon train?"

"That's what I been saying. Whar is Moose?"

"He go."

"Then I'll just have to bring ye the word myself. It's off. The raid is off. Crawford and his volunteers— You savvy Crawford?" He knew by their expressions that indeed they did savvy Crawford, whose group of volunteers had lately cleared the Bannocks and Cheyennes from the South Pass. "Many men. Mountain guns. Cannon. German repeaters. Dead Injuns."

The scarface said, "No, Crawford south, many sleeps."

"All right. I'll not argue with ye. It's your grave if ye want to fill it. Done my part. Brought ye the warning like Hames asked. So now I'll just be gittin' back."

"No," said the scarface. "You stop."

Against the side of his head was something cold and hard. He stiffened. He turned his head slowly and looked down the barrel of a Jaeger rifle.

The scarface with a crafty look in his one eye said, "You wait. Maybe you sneak up, listen? Maybe not. We send, find out."

Comanche John did not argue with the scarface—or the Jaeger. He let them take his guns and walk him inside the house, down a hall, and inside a tiny, thick-walled, windowless room. They locked the door. He was alone in the darkness.

He sat down. He dozed and awakened, and dozed again. It was daylight now—he could see glints of the sky through the shake-covered poles that formed the roof.

To pass the time, he examined the room. It had served as a powder lockup back in the fur-trade days. The door was heavy, whipsawed plank, double-thick, held by a heavy bar on the outside. The pole flooring was loose, merely flattened on two sides and laid into place, but the room had its own rock foundation as a precaution against a fire creeping beneath to the powder kegs. The walls had been hewn smooth, the logs set flush one against the other, leaving no place for a finger- or toehold, and the heavy pole members of the roof would be immovable anyway. It was an excellent prison. He sat back again, leaned against a wall; he chawed and waited.

He could hear the Indians arguing horses. He learned by listening that the scarfaced one was named Kinepah. John had heard a great deal about Kinepah. Kinepah was one of the Palouse chiefs in on the Steptoe massacre of '58; he had escaped later from the Indian defeat at Four Lakes and had been on the loose ever since. With this being Kinepah, the younger Palouse was probably Deerskin Shirt, and the oldest man, the taciturn fullblood with the roached hair, was Three Horse, who had been in trouble with white men since the Cayuse War back in '48.

"What a fine crew that Hames *has* tied himself up with!" he said. What a fine crew, indeed! Why, these renegades would use Hames as much as they could, and when that point was reached he'd be just another white man. They'd end up by riding off with his hair on their medicine sticks.

CHAPTER SEVEN

THERE HAD BEEN NO NECESSITY for John covering his trail the night he departed from the wagon train. Ambrose Stocker returned, furious over the manner in which he had been treated. There had been another powwow at which it was decided that they *should* form a posse and run him down and hang him, but nobody, not even Hames, was willing to actually saddle and start out. No one got much sleep. In the morning, the Parson conducted the burial of Joe Wood. It was a brief service, but even before its conclusion some of the wagons had started to move on. Courteous and sympathetic, Hames came to Lela, holding his hat across his breast, and asked with humble earnestness for the privilege of driving her wagon. Rusty had not been seen since the night before, so she consented.

She kept watching for Rusty. Concerning his disappearance, she was alternately apprehensive and bitter. Common belief was that he had ridden off with Comanche John. He was a coward, Mrs. Stocker said, and had had some hand in the killing. Otherwise, why hadn't he even been there for the service? On the other hand, the Parson cast hints of a plot that went much deeper than any of them imagined.

"You wait," he said to her. "You just wait till all the facts are in. Comanche John had no part of that shooting. Nor Rusty, neither."

It was hard to believe him with everyone saying the opposite. At best, at very best, Rusty was a coward. She told herself that she hated him.

They fought the road. It had reached such a state that a crew had to go ahead to roll boulders and chop windfalls from the way. They made barely half a mile an hour. Late in the afternoon Stocker rode down the grade, encouraging them, saying, "Camp ahead. Keep going, grass ahead. Big Hole turnoff. It looks good. Keep going, grass ahead."

The turnoff did look good after the road they had been following. It slanted off into the timber, narrow but smooth, a steady climb.

Belly River Bob, standing by a fire, pointed it out to each traveler as he pulled in, saying, "There she is. Good road. Steady pull. Road to the gold fields. Road to the White Pine, too, if you'd rather."

They had supper, and then a meeting with Stocker in charge. Only the Parson spoke against the turnoff, and it was noted that he did it without his usual spirit, and when he had finished he did not even wait for the voting, knowing what it would be, but went to his wagon to brood.

There, later that night, Betsy Cobb found him.

"Big Hole?" he asked.

"Yes. Well, you can't blame 'em."

"No, we can't blame 'em."

"But that's not what worries me. Not the main thing."

"What, then?"

"Lela."

He guessed the worst. "She's going to marry him—that Hames?"

"So she says."

Betsy waited for the Parson to do something, but all he could do was hold his head, rock back and forth on his stool, and speak of fate.

The wagon train was badly beaten out; it was voted to lay over for grass and repairs. In the afternoon, Mrs. Shallerbach and Mrs. Stocker took charge of the wedding and moved everything out of the Stocker wagon except for a small table which they decorated with their best fancywork, making an altar. While this was going on, Betsy appeared once more at the Parson's wagon.

She stood with hands on hips and said, "You ain't takin' a part in this thing, are you?"

"What thing?"

"The wedding."

"I haven't been out of the wagon except for a bucket of water. I—"

"I mean, you aren't performing the ceremony."

"Such things ain't of the minister's choosing."

"Oh, thunder! You mean you *would* marry 'em?"

"The gal is free to choose. I might advise, but if she says he's the man of her choice, then—"

"He kilt Joe Wood."

"You can't prove he did."

"He *kilt* him. You know it and I know it. And yet, in spite of that, and that poor, fatherless lamb out there, you'd use your ordained blessing to tie 'em up in matrimony."

"Sister Cobb, if I didn't, then Stocker would. He has the right, recognized by law, the leader of a wagon train, just like the captain of a ship at sea."

"Oh, you make my gorge rise," she said, and stomped outside.

"Alas," said the Parson to the cold and empty wagon. "I can't fight 'em alone. What's an old rooster like me going to do?"

He remained so, without moving, for almost an hour, until someone rapped at the door.

"Come in," he said.

It was Mrs. Dilworth. She looked taller than usual. She was gaunt and shaky.

"I had my hand in something terrible," she blurted out. "I did. I'm certain of it. I had my hand in murder."

The Parson showed life. "Where? Joe Woods?"

"Yes. I was going to my wagon when Wally Snite— I never did trust him, I never trusted a man with pale eyes—"

"What about Snite?"

"He said Joe Wood wanted to see John, so I told him, and they kilt him. I'm sure of it. They kilt him and laid it to John. I had my hand in murder. Why am I so sure? I'll tell you—because if John was on the kill would he wait to be sent for?"

The Parson questioned her, but she had no proof.

"Don't you believe me?" she wailed.

"Yes, *I* believe it, but would *anybody else* believe? You go along and say nothing. I got to think about what to do."

The Parson did think about it, and about himself, alone in his weakness. He made up his mind what to do. First he must stop the wedding. He went to bed. He moaned. It was half an hour before one of the Orham kids heard him. The Parson sent him for help. Help came in the person of Betsy Cobb, who begged him to recognize her, to rise up for just one second and *say* so before he slipped over to Beulah Land.

The Parson gasped for Lela Wood, and the Orham kid sped away for her, and she came running, holding her borrowed wedding dress up away from the juniper.

"He's nigh gone," whispered Betsy Cobb, meeting her at the door. "Oh-h, I could see it coming. And I talked to him so, only two hours past. Oh-h! How can I ever forgive myself?"

"Parson!" Lela said, on her knees beside his bed.

"Who is it?" gasped the Parson. "I heared the voice of an angel. Be I in heaven already?"

"You aren't going to die, Parson. You aren't!"

"Oh, yes, child! But I'll be a happy corpse. I will now that you're here to promise me one thing—"

"You're not." She looked up and saw Betsy and two other women just arrived, standing there. "Get some water heated. Heat up some stones. Blankets. And some whisky. Is there any left?"

The Parson said, "No use wasting likker on me. My earthly race is run. In My Father's house thar is many mansions, as the Good Book says, and I'll soon be trading this here ornery old prairie schooner for one of 'em."

She held his hand and whispered, "No, no!"

Ague seized him and he shook all over so Lela had to keep putting the quilts back on him. "One last wish. It's for you, gal!"

"Yes!"

"I had a awful premonition. Don't go through with that wedding. Don't let any captain of any wagon train marry you after I'm gone, neither. I had a vision. Balls of fire and lakes of brimstone descending on this wagon train I seen if you did. Corpses and charred remains. Promise you'll not get married until you get to White Pine."

"I won't, Parson. I won't!"

"Ah!" sighed the Parson, and subsided with hands folded across his breast.

"Is he gone? Is he gone?" asked the Widow Cobb. "Glory to his sainted memory, is he gone? Do you reckon we ought to lay him out in his old black serge, or would you say his frock coat and gaiters? And a coffin! I say *this* time we must have a coffin."

The Parson, with one eye open, whispered, "Don't rush me, Sister Cobb. Don't rush me."

The wedding was postponed. All night, with women hovering close, the Parson clung to life.

CHAPTER EIGHT

AT THE MOMENT the Parson was gasping his last request to Lela Wood, Comanche John was seated in the darkness of the old powder room, chawing and spitting, still listening to the interminable Indian argument concerning horses. Then, to busy himself, he once more groped the room with the thought of escape.

The flooring again interested him. The rock foundation of the room was a hopeless barrier, but something else occurred to him. It made him spit hard and chuckle and say, "Why, damme, yes!" He could move some of the poles near the door, lie flat on the ground with the poles over him, and present an empty room to the eyes of the first man who came to look for him.

He had to lie on his back, full length, and in that position it was not easy to replace the pole flooring over him, but he did it, and settled himself for a long wait. The ground was cold but not uncomfortable. Much superior to his porch beam of the night before. He even dozed a little.

He awakened with a start. The voices had taken on a new pitch. Someone had just arrived—the messenger sent to talk to Lawford Hames. And a few seconds later he heard, *felt*, the approach of moccasined feet.

The feet paused. The door was being unbarred. It was pulled open—lifted and dragged. The man was very close, almost atop him. He could feel the sink of floor poles just above his knees. He lay rigid, not breathing.

"Ho!" the man said, looking into the room. "Ho! Come on, see chief."

It was the Palouse, Deerskin Shirt. He had moved enough now so John could see him through a crack between two poles. He was in the door, crouched, a rifle aimed, peering around the dark room.

"Ho!" he said again, this time with alarm. He realized that the room was empty. He burst in to look around for a hole in the walls or ceiling. He had stopped in the middle of the room. John lifted one of the floor poles. His head moved up, above the level of the floor. The Indian was only a long step away, his back turned. John's chance was now.

He sprang, hurling the floor poles away from him. The Indian started to turn. There was no time for it. John had him, right hand grasping the back of his capote jacket, his left arm bent around his throat.

The Indian was off balance, staggering. He stopped among loosened floor poles and tried to dump John over his head, but John was ready for the maneuver. It was a silent struggle across the room, the Indian young, tough, and quick, but unable to break the power of the bent arm which cut off his breath.

They fell to the floor. John still held him. He waited as the Indian's struggles became futile and stopped, and he waited a while yet.

He listened. No one coming. They still talked loudly in the far room. He stood up, found the Indian's gun, a smooth-bore double pistol loaded with buckshot, checked to make sure of the load, and, with gun in hand, stepped from the door.

He was in a short hallway. He still had to go through the big room, and there were men there, six of them.

He walked very quietly. He had a look. A candle burned above the fireplace; rifles leaned against the wall; rifles lay on the table; his own Navies were also on the table, still in their holsters, belts wrapped around them. There was one-eyed Kinepah with his back to him, talking in the Palouse tongue, gesturing his thoughts out in the sign language.

John kept walking. He walked straight into the room. The Indians and breeds were all listening to Kinepah. John had to nudge one of them out of the way. He glanced at John without seeming to realize who he was. John was then at the table. He picked up his Navies. He tossed the belts and holsters over his left arm and turned just as Kinepah, recognizing him, cried, "*E-e Ya!*"

John moved with a spring and half-pivot, stopping at a crouch with his back to the door. He shouted, "No, ye don't!"

They froze, staring into the twin muzzles of the gun —all save one half-breed who ducked to the floor and tried to come up unseen beneath the table with a rifle.

John pulled one of the triggers. The pistol roared, filling the room with its concussion. The half-breed, hit at close range by the charge of buckshot, was knocked to his back. Now they were all after their guns, a mad charge of men inside the small quarters. John fired again. He swung the empty pistol at a man who tried to get in his way. He dived headlong through the door, rolled over on the packed earth outside, made it to his feet again, and ran.

Bullets roared around him. A bullet tore splinters from one of the porch poles. He was in the open. On a path through snow. He abandoned it for a short-cut to timber. He waded drifts. He fell and crawled. He came up amid scrub timber. He ran again. He found a path. He slowed, getting his wind, taking time to buckle on his Navies.

He kept going. His jackboots were not made for running. His foot wrappings, worn in substitute for socks, had worked down, making uncomfortable lumps above his heels and under his insteps so that he felt clubfooted. They were filled with snow. He wanted to stop and fix things, but he did not dare. He kept going, up and on until at last, on the steep slope of the mountain, he lost his pursuers, at least momentarily, and sat down.

He got his wind, took off his boots, emptied them of half-melted snow, rewrapped his feet, and got the boots on again. All that took time, maybe five minutes, and all the while he kept watch to see how the pursuit was organizing.

Someone was trailing him straight through the snow. Others, on horseback, were circling, ready to close in on him whenever he was located.

He climbed on over the ridge and dropped down into the little parklike area where he had left his horse.

"Here, pony," he said. "You still thar, pony?"

He had a bad few seconds, then a movement revealed the animal, waiting with head up in the shadow blackness of fir trees.

"Why, sure," said John, "thar ye be," and went to work blanketing and saddling him.

Riders crested the ridge an eighth of a mile to his left. He could see them, one after another, against the stars. Five.

"Hey-ya!" came a voice from the other direction.

"Ya!" one of the riders answered.

They kept calling and answering in a Palouse jargon that John was unfamiliar with, but the trackers were still over the ridge, and he was certain the others had not located him.

He mounted and rode, following a route through timber. The darkness hid him, but it was slow. He fended branches with hands and arms, keeping them from his face. The timber ended, and he was on a second ridge.

No sign of them now. He reached for his chewing tobacco. Then suddenly: *"Hey-ya!"* The voice of an Indian split the quiet not fifty paces away, and suddenly they were on him from two sides.

He quirted the gunpowder to a gallop. He rode recklessly downhill, across rocks and windfalls. Someone shot at him, but it was wild. He was in timber and out again. Ahead of him yawned a black abyss. It was a deep gulch. He followed a deer trail. It took him over the brink. He rode down and down, switchback, and after an hour he reached the bottom, where an icy little stream flowed through rocks and new snow.

He listened. For a long time there had been no sound of pursuit. There was none now. He was shut of them. He rode on as dawn came, and he was still riding when the sun rose, shining pink and yellow on cliffs a thousand feet above.

It took more hours before a trail climbed from the gulch. At noon he reached some shelf rock from which the country was visible. All was unfamiliar. He rode northward, knowing that somewhere in that direction lay the Big Hole trail.

He circled a mountain, topped another ridge, and from there, looking far across a V-shaped gulch, he saw the moving shapes of wagons.

The sun was bright, melting the snow, and where there was grass it looked almost green. The scene, with the covered wagons and all, had a picture-book quality that reassured him. He decided there was no hurry after all. He rode along the ridge, descending little by little, keeping just even with the wagons, until he was startled to hear his name called.

"John!"

It was Rusty. He rode toward John from the gulch, bareback, hatless, guiding his pony by means of a rope hackamore. He had been wounded on the head, he had bled a great deal, his hair was a solid mass of hardened blood. A purplish bruise extended down his left temple across his cheek; his eye was swollen shut. He carried his right arm in a peculiar manner close against his stomach.

"Lad, what the devil?"

"It was that night, that same night, they laid in wait."

"For you? Who laid in wait?"

"I think Belly River Bob. He come up behind me, it was so quick, and next thing I knew I was down among the rocks. I knew he was above, waiting for me to move, so I just laid there. Finally I crawled away. Daylight before I could walk. Dizzy. Broke my arm. I followed the wagon train, but Sanchez was rear sentry. He'd have killed me. Finally this horse strayed. Lafe's horse." Then he said defensively, raising his voice, "You think I'm a coward. I'm not! I'll git a gun and go back after those—"

"No, now! You think because you git *scared* you're a coward? It's what a man does spite of being scared tells whether he's a coward. We better look at the arm."

But John had no time to examine the arm. A movement far across and below caught his eyes. He stopped and watched. A man was climbing on foot from the creek bottom toward a steep pitch where the road made a switchback about a mile's travel ahead of the lead wagon. The man was perfectly visible from John's position, but he could not be seen from the road where the wagon train would soon be creeping past. There was a second flicker of movement—a second man. Then a third, this one above the road, and there was gun shine, its exact position hard to determine.

"Ambush!" muttered Comanche John.

"Who?" cried Rusty. "Where?"

John waved him quiet. He had no time to answer questions. "You got a gun? No. Waal, you stay back. Yes, I tell ye to stay back. I got a job to do."

Turning his horse, he rode steeply down the slope.

CHAPTER NINE

ALL MORNING the Widow Cobb had driven the Parson's wagon. Now it was midday, with the sun shining warm, melting the snow, and the wagon train was headed steeply up the Big Hole road.

When the jouncing got so bad the Parson was unable to stay in bed, he got up, and holding to one thing and another, reached the front of the wagon where he looked through the drawstring aperture. He had been there a minute or so before the Widow glanced around and saw him.

"Git back to bed!" she cried. "Oh, mercy me, he's walking in delirium. I shouldn't have left the poor creetur alone."

"I'm in no delirium," said the Parson. "In fact, I believe some of the poisons have been jounced out of me. I feel a mite recovered."

"Oh, don't you believe it. You look pale as a ghost newrisen by moonlight. Just like my man, that poor, sainted Mr. Cobb, up one minute with a talk of fixing harness, and not three hour later stiff, stark, and turning cold."

He said, a trifle testily, "Aren't you pushing a trifle hard for such an old contraption as this?"

"Orders. Hames, Ambrose Stocker, I don't argue. This be the fate of us poor helpless women, just be meek, don't argue with the menfolk, git along the best we can."

High on the rocks, a mile ahead, rode a single brief glimmer of metal. It could have been Belly River Bob riding scout, but the Parson was brought up sharp with suspicion.

"Any hint of Injun trouble?"

She looked surprised. "Why?"

"Nothing, nothing at all, but I'll hold those reins while you go and fetch O'Donnell."

She got down and stood beside the road as two outfits creaked past. The third was O'Donnell's.

She called up that the Parson wanted to see him, so he handed the lines to his wife and climbed down, all without stopping the wagon, and walked forward with Betsy, past the other outfits, and without the necessity of hurrying, they were moving that slow.

"What's the trouble?" he asked.

"Gun shine."

"Where?"

She pointed up the mountain ahead. "I told him it

was probably Bob or Sanchez, but you know how he worries, Injun behind every rock and the devil himself in the timber."

A couple of others had seen the gun shine, and the sight of O'Donnell and Betsy walking to the Parson's wagon sent a word of alarm down the line. Someone stopped, halting the wagons behind, and soon the entire train had come to a standstill.

Big Lawford Hames now came riding along the narrow shelf at the edge of the road, demanding what the trouble was.

"Gun shine be damned!" he said. "That's our own scout. Come on and roll!"

But the Parson was out of his wagon, leaving it to block the way, and was jerking the inside front wheel back and forth.

"Now what the hell?" said Hames. "I thought you were sick."

"I got to pull this wheel."

"Get up there! Get to rolling."

"No!" The Parson faced him like a gaunt, long-necked rooster. "I got a sprung wheel; I don't want it to be a broke wheel."

Hames knew there was nothing more than ordinary wrong with the wheel. In fury he brought his horse around, trying to pin the Parson against the side of the wagon. When that failed he swung a brutal forearm blow to the side of the old man's neck.

The Parson went down, doubled over in the rocks and dirt. Betsy Cobb shouted in dismay and started to jerk her double pistol, but Hames, making another pivot with his horse, smashed it from her hand.

The Parson's team took fright and lunged, threatening to take wagon and all over the edge of the bank. Betsy abandoned her gun while going for the reins and the brake. O'Donnell, unarmed, picked up a rock, and Hames, not hesitating, rode him down.

"I said *roll!*" Hames shouted in a rage-hoarse voice. "Keep the wagons together. Roll!"

O'Donnell staggered to his feet. In falling he had

knocked his head against a rock, but the horse had missed stepping on him. He saw the Parson still down and picked him up. The Parson suddenly came to life and tried to get loose. He kicked and waved his arms, he flopped around like a decapitated chicken, but O'Donnell held him.

"Be still," said O'Donnell. "I'll get you to your wagon."

"I don't want to be got to my wagon. Let me go. Get guns. Stop the lead wagon. Make circle."

"On this mountain road? Everything will be all right."

"No, they won't be. There's something wrong. I knew it when they kilt Joe Wood and drove off John, all to get us strung out here on the Big Hole Pass."

O'Donnell managed to keep hold of him. He ran the last few steps and with a Herculean effort dropped him over the endgate into the wagon.

In the distance a gun exploded. There came another shot, then a scattering volley. A voice, Comanche John's, came from deep in the gulch: "*Injun! Ya-hoo, Injun!*"

"Injun! Injun!" echoed the Widow Cobb.

Hames went gray-faced at the disruption of his plans. He spurred his big bay horse up the road along-side the wagons, calling, "Nothing to fear. Some damn fool's trying to scare you. Those are peaceful Nez Percés. Nothing to fear. They could cut us to pieces, but I have them bought off. Whatever you do, don't fire a shot. Kippen, put that rifle down. Don't shoot. I'll get you through. Do as I say, I'll get you through."

"You mean drive right into 'em?" Lafe called. "Like hell. Up there they'll have us above and below. *Here* we can fight for it."

"Keep going!" Hames cried.

"No."

Hames lifted his pistol. "I said keep going!"

But Lafe was under the edge of the wagon box. "No, damn you, I'm not moving another inch."

A wagoner saw someone high on the slope and fired. A volley came from above and below. Shallerbach was on the ground. His wife and the Nelson boy were dragging him to cover in the wagon. Others maneuvered their teams, producing tangles with other outfits on the narrow road. A team bolted. The wagon went over the edge. It jackknifed and turned over with a crash, spilling supplies down the mountain. A flour barrel rolled for a hundred yards, leaped high, and split itself with a puff of white.

"Against the bank!" Dilworth was shouting. "Pull in against the bank."

Most wagons found partial cover there. The shooting, after the first flurry, had almost stopped.

Hames rode directly into the open, his beaver hat lifted high, signaling to the ambushers to cease fire, signaling back to the wagons to show how safe it was. He wanted all the shooting to stop. He called to Stocker, telling him to come, to bring the men, all of them, to set their brakes and leave their wagons, and come on in a group, and parley with the Indians. But Stocker hesitated.

"Once he gets you up there," called Betsy, "you'll never see your wagons again. What a sweet way for him to get back in the freight business, with *our* stock and wagons, yes, and make himself a hero besides."

"That's damn-foolery," said Stocker, but just the same he did not leave his outfit.

An Indian or a breed, trying to edge from one rock to another, was hit by a long-range bullet from Kippen's rifle. He lay calling for help, and that was enough to start his companions shooting in earnest. They advanced from above and below, and the wagoners, from the precarious cover afforded by the road, made it hot for them.

The Parson was down on one knee, an old-time flintlock conversion in his hands, its long barrel poked through a hole in the wagon box, aiming and firing and shouting, "More powder and ball!" to the Widow Cobb.

"Gimme that gun! Go to bed where you belong."

"Powder and ball! They're closing in." Then he listened. Over the shooting and shouting came a voice he recognized. "It's him, it's him!" He hopped to his feet and did a spindly-legged war dance. "Do ye hear it? It's the Comanche! It's Comanche John! We'll tear 'em asunder now, Sister Cobb!"

"Lord help us, you mean Smith *is* Comanche John?"

"He's a ring-tailed ripper from the Rawhide Mountains. And oh, am I thankful to Leviticus I didn't convert him into laying down his Navies! The trick in this preaching, Sister Cobb, is to convert 'em just so far they ain't varmints and not so far as to make 'em useless."

CHAPTER TEN

AFTER A WILD DESCENT through the brush of a gully, Comanche John reached the creek bottom. Rusty, clinging to the neck of his horse, was close on his heels. There they left their horses and climbed on foot. The wagon train was partly halted, and for a moment John thought he might yet reach it before it passed into the range of the ambush, but the lead wagons were moving again, so he fired to warn them.

He hardly expected one bullet to do the business, but it did. A breed, crouched a couple-hundred paces up the slope, tense on the trigger, fired from nervousness. Seconds later everyone seemed to be shooting.

"Injun!" John whooped through cupped hands. "Yahoo, Injun!"

"Injun! Injun!" he heard the Widow Cobb saying.

Shooting from everywhere now. John crawled up the slope, through scrub bushes, over rocks. He saw the upset wagon, the puff of white as the flour barrel burst. He saw Hames ride into the open, signaling with his hat. He could hear nothing that was said.

Then shooting again. High on the slope, someone was wounded. John kept climbing. He was almost up to the main ambush position. Kinepah was calling orders, this man by name, and that one, then he heard Hames and the voice of Belly River Bob.

"Hold your shooting!" Hames said. He did not shout, but his voice carried. "Hold up! Take that bulge of ground. Then we'll work both ways."

The bulge he referred to was a shoulder of the mountain. Taking that would cut the train in half; a dozen rifles at that point could cut it to pieces.

Kinepah, in the jargon, relayed the orders. The shooting petered out. John took the opportunity to reload the empty cylinder in his gun. He did it while climbing over rocks and windfalls, getting closer, and a little closer yet.

He could see eight or nine men and guess the positions of others. No one looked at him. If they noticed his movement, they thought him one of their own.

A half-breed, trigger-nervous, fired at something uphill. "Wait up, wait up!" called Belly River Bob.

"No, don't wait up," John bellowed. "The time is now."

He rose. Belly River Bob, in scrub timber, looked directly down on him. He lifted his gun, but John's double blast from the Navies hit him, doubling him in the middle, so that he fired at his own boot toes.

He still had enough left to crawl on his stomach. John was busy elsewhere. He turned, firing as men scattered for cover. One, running, he got beautifully like a bird on the wing, but another, a sitting duck, he should have had, but unaccountably his bullet went wild.

An answering shot plucked at his buckskin jacket. Another pounded slivers of rock that stung him. He got down and crawled. He came up firing both pistols and dived again. His guns empty, he stopped, back against a ten-foot boulder, reloaded.

There was Rusty, gunless, trying to follow him.

"Git down or git kilt!" John said. "What do ye aim to do, not even a gun? Throw rocks at 'em?"

"I'm no coward."

"You've proved that. Git down. Wave your shirt."

Rusty stripped off his shirt, fastened it to a dead branch, and lifted it, drawing shots from eight or ten directions, allowing John to circle higher, and then catch them from an unexpected angle and send them scattering again.

"Yipee!" said John, pouring bullets up the slope. "I'm a ring-tailed ripper from the Rawhide Mountains. I pepper my taters with gunpowder and I eat my meat with the hair on. I kill me a man each day of the year and two on Jeff Davis's birthday just to be patriotic. Yipee! I got graveyards named after me all the way from Fraser River to Yuba Gulch, I have for a fact, and it's my fancy to commence another one on this side hill."

Kinepah came down the slope, snaking himself on his belly, and bobbed into view with a rifle, to be met and smashed backward by a cross-body shot from John's right-hand Navy. With their leader gone, the others took to cover, every man for himself, looking only for horses and escape. Higher, about the trail, the wagoners had the others in flight. It had become sniping from long range and a plain waste of bullets.

John stood now, and climbed. He found Belly River Bob shot through both legs and groaning. "Don't shoot. I done nothing to you. I'm a wounded man."

"Whar's Hames?"

"Gone." Bob named him something suitable and vile. "Gone and left me. Turned yellow. Headed for Montana Territory. You patch me up, don't let them farmers hang me, and I'll follow him. I'll git him."

"No, *I'll* git him. I wouldn't want to cheat those good Pikes Peakers out of the joy of a hanging. Getting *him* is a job I fancy for myself."

Hours later, toward sunset, all the wagons finally got turned in the narrow road and commenced rolling back toward the forks, it having been voted not to take the Big Hole trail after all, but to proceed to the Bitterroot. Rusty, with his head bandaged and his broken arm in splints and a sling, sat beside Lela in the high seat of her wagon, their shoulders touching, neither of them speaking, their happiness too complete. The Parson in his wagon kept craning around at each bend, trying to glimpse them, saying, "Yep, yep! I *will* have a marriage to perform."

"You might have a double marriage to perform," said the Widow Cobb significantly. "Yes, you just might."

The wagons camped at the old place near the forks, but Comanche John was not there for supper. Later, after the camp was quiet, the Parson roused in the darkness of his wagon and found him rummaging the food can for cold biscuits.

"What's the matter with you?" he asked. "You don't have to sneak in here. Ain't a man on this wagon train would hang you now."

"I'm not afeared of hanging. Ropes nor guns nor the hatchets of the Sioux hold no fear for me. It's that woman out thar. She's enamored of me."

"Betsy?"

"Yes, Betsy."

"Well, John," the Parson said gently, laying a hand on his arm, "it might just be for the best. She'd make a good wife for you."

"No, Parson." Revealed by moonlight through the rear door of the wagon, Comanche John looked popeyed as the Parson had never seen him. "There's something about that woman. The way she *looks* at me. Always up and down and across like she war measuring me for a coffin."

"Oh, John, that's plain foolishness."

"It ain't! She buried one husband already. And do you know what she said to me one time? Without warning she said, 'Brother John, do you own a black serge suit?' No, Parson. This is as far as I go. I got ye to the Bitterroot. Close enough, anyhow. Tonight I'm riding on. Over the big ridge. It's Montana for me. And Hames—I'll find him thar. He kilt Joe Wood, as fine a man as I ever met. He struck you, Parson, and I don't tolerate that, either. I got a score to settle with him."

"That's no Christian attitude," the Parson tried to tell him, but John, his mouth and pockets full of cold biscuit, was already lowering himself over the endgate to the ground.

"Waal, I'll convert him. I'll give him twelve good argyments, six with each hand."

His gunpowder pony was waiting, and through the chill mountain air the Parson could hear the squeak of saddle leather as he mounted, the click of hoofs on stones as he started off at an easy amble, the sort of pace a man takes when he aims to ride a long, far piece before next bed-down, and John's singing voice, a monotone, the words bumped from him by the movements of the horse—

> "Oh, gather 'round, ye teamster men,
>   And listen to my tale
> Of Comanche John the highwayman
>   Who rides the outlaw trail;
> Upon his head an old slouch hat
>   And boots above the knee,
> A rougher, tougher woolly-wolf
>   Ye seldom ever see."

CHAPTER ELEVEN

HE RODE ALL NIGHT. He stopped high on a wintry pass to tramp life into his feet. Behind him, misty and vast, was Idaho; ahead of him, in great summits and purple-timbered canyons, he could see a hundred miles as the bird flew. Well, John was no bird and he was not riding one, and it would be a tough, long ride across the flanks of the Bitterroots. And Bannock was too well supplied with hangrope, anyhow.

"Poor scratch camp," he muttered. "Ain't up to a man o' my style."

He avoided Proctor Diggings, too, figuring Hames might go there, and Sanchez and Little Tom with him. Only Petley was killed in the fight or, at least, so one of those Pikes Peakers had claimed.

He wanted a run-in with Hames, of course. He was *looking* for Hames, and would settle with him, but all at a time of John's choosing, and not in Proctor where a vigilance committee might be stirred up.

He slept in a spruce-branch lean-to far over on the Montana side. He developed a horse croup bordering on pneumonia and stopped at an Indian trader's, where he spent a week in and out of bed, doctoring himself with an Indian remedy consisting of stewed camas and whisky. A heavy snowfall came and melted off. The weather turned balmy as summer all over again. He prospected some little gulches. He followed a stream northward, panning and sampling the outcroppings as he went. He crossed a pass where snow reached the belly of his horse. He shacked up with seven prospectors in one tiny cabin through a big blizzard and the cold afterward. By Christmas he had a strong hankering for polka music, and proceeded on to Carolina Gulch where he lost everything, even his horse and bedroll, playing faro.

He left town on foot; it was not his fault that his pony got loose and followed him. Of course, he had hired a hostler at the stable to *turn* him loose, but following him had been the pony's own idea. Anyhow, he had a suspicion that the faro game was crooked. Riding again, John 'lowed he should go back and shoot that crooked faro dealer, but he didn't. He rode on to the camp of Apex, which lay on flat ground, over the headwaters of Grindstone River. Apex he found ravaged by an epidemic of horse croup that had already claimed the lives of seven.

He set up in business manufacturing his remedy of camas and trade liquor, and produced some spectacular cures, until the camp's leading citizen, president of the miners' meeting, a man very highly thought of, drank an entire week's course of treatment in a single night and staggered off on one of the side trails to freeze to death.

This produced some ugly talk, so John sold out to a Chinaman and departed, ending the winter at a Flathead Indian village north of Hell Gate.

Come spring, he went prospecting. He failed to turn even a color. He traveled south again, partly to see the Parson and learn how his emigrants had fared at White Pine Valley, but mostly because of a recent stampede to some new diggings at near-by Shauvegan Gulch.

His horse went lame. He left him with a French-Cree rancher and went in style on the coach.

The coach driver was a tall, loose, red-mustached man much fortified by three big slugs from the station keeper's bottle.

"It's ho! for the gold fields of Shauvegan Gulch, El Dorado, and the Chiny Diggings," he whooped, climbing to the high seat. "So git aboard or git left behind because I'm a timely man and this coach is an hour late already."

Ten passengers packed themselves inside. John wanted none of *that*. He climbed to the hurricane where he sat with his feet between the guard and the driver.

"Ya-hoo!" the driver shouted. He barely waited for the last passenger to get inside. He kicked the brake, signaled for the lead team to be let loose, and came down swinging his long lash. The horses, fresh for the pull up Moosehorn Pass, responded by almost jumping out of their hides. They were off at a run with the coach wildly careening behind them. Never were more than three of the coach's wheels on earth at once, and at times not any, but still the whooping driver urged them on; on top Comanche John and the guard held tight and rode well enough, but the inside was a scramble of cursing humanity.

After half a mile, with some of the vinegar burned from his horses, the driver eased back, handling each animal just so with his double-handful of ribbons until they were all pulling right and the coach rocking as easy as a hammock.

They entered a deep gulch with forested mountains rising to bald pinnacles on each side. Here were evening shadows, and an evening chill sharpened by the fragrance of pine. John shivered and tied the fastenings of his buckskin jacket.

"Been to Blackfoot City," he remarked. "Thar and Hell Gate. Too much high life. Nigh the finish of me. Regular meals, sleeping in a bed—I tell ye, it softens a man up. All very well when you're young, but when ye git to crowding forty, *no*. Especially when you're crowding it the wrong way." He hitched his Navy Colts to more comfortable positions, aimed a spurt of tobacco juice at some rocks projecting from one side of the road, and asked, "At what o'clock will ye raise the Chiny Diggings?"

"Midnight. Unless we have to swim the Sulphurwater. That's the *diggings,* though. You're bound for New Boston. New Boston is five-six mile farther along."

The coach splashed across a shallow stream and started upgrade on a road dug from the loose sand-rock of the mountain. Making himself comfortable with one boot on the brake, the driver rolled his eye at the shotgun guard and added, "Yep, midnight, *if* we don't meet up with road agents."

The guard, heavy-set and truculent, said, "This is an *in*coming coach. Who the hell would be crazy enough to rob an *in*coming one?"

"Did at the Yallerstone this spring. Banks in the country now. Banks bring in greenbacks. And I hear that Comanche John has moved in here from Idaho."

The guard knew he was being needled, but he could not help bristling back. "I hope that braggart *does* try to rob my outfit sometime. I only *hope so*." He whacked the eight-gauge shotgun between his knees. "Because if he does I'll hit him with a quarter-pound of number-two buck and turn him so the hair side's in."

The black-whiskered man on the hurricane said, "Co-man-che? Ye mean he's an Injun?"

"No. Pike County white man, if you can call Missourians *white*. Dirty, bushwhacking, killing, robbing —"

The driver said, "Robs from the rich and gives to the poor."

"Hah!"

Whereupon the driver got his chew of tobacco off to one side and lifted his voice in song:

> *"Thar's a forty-dozen highwaymen*
> *'Twixt Denver and the sea,*
> *But I sing of old Comanche John*
> *The fastest gun thar be;*
> *He robs the bank, he robs the stage,*
> *And what's a dang site more,*
> *He takes that misbegotten wealth*
> *And give it to the pore."*

The black-whiskered man said, "That was *purty*. Would ye mind singing on a bit?"

The guard shouted, "No, don't sing any more! That damn song'll end by driving me crazy. Anyhow, it don't make no never-mind because the Comanche is dead. I heared it that he was hung by the vigilantes over in I-de-ho City."

"That's what I heared, too!" said the black-whiskered one. "He's low in his grave so nobody needs to be looking for him, and that's a relief. That *is* a relief!" To prove what a relief it was he removed his black slouch hat to wipe away some imaginary perspiration. "But I *would* like to hear some more of that song."

So the driver tuned himself with a couple of false starts and sang:

"Co-man-che rode to Yallerjack
On the twelfth day of July,
With chawin' tobacca in his mouth
And killin' in his eye,
Upon his head an old slouch hat
And boots above the knee,
A faster shootin' highwayman
You seldom ever see.

"Now Co-man-che had a pardner
By the name of Whisky Ike,
And the only motto that they had
Was share and share alike;
They robbed the coach at Uniontown
They robbed the—"

"Quit it, quit that caterwauling," cried the guard. "I got to look and listen both on this job."

The driver still ruminated the song under his breath for a while, then he said to the black-whiskered man, "I don't want to be misunderstood, but how the Comanche is described in that song *does* cut you right down the middle."

"I'm just a poor pilgrim on the trail of life," John said sanctimoniously. "Brown's the handle. John Brown, and no relation to that varmint they hung at Harper's Ferry. Besides, as ye say, the Comanche is low in his grave at I-de-ho City—"

"They hung him in Yankee Flats and in Placerville, too. By grab, I never see a man that was hung so often as that Comanche John." He rolled an eye on the jittery guard. "How about you, McQueen? Ever see a man hung so many times and still turn up again?"

"If he tries to rob this coach there'll be no need to hang him."

There followed a long, slow pull. Darkness had almost settled when they reached the crest of the pass. A glow from the west revealed a vast timber and mountain country, the snowy summits of the Gold Creek Range to the northeast, and straight away, some miles below, a twinkling cluster of lights.

"New Boston?" asked the whiskered man.

"No, New Boston is hid in the gulch. That's the Irish Bar, a bench placer. Torchlight, work night and day. Git the gold out fast and turn the country back to the Injuns, that's the ticket!"

The coach entered timber and started down a steep drop with the brakes rubbing. It was very dark there. The driver had a hard time keeping his leaders moving fast enough, while the swing team, more than willing now that the pull was over, threatened to tangle the harness. There was a sharp turn, and the leaders suddenly came to a stop with the other horses all crowding them.

The driver cursed fluently, managing the lines with one hand and putting his weight on the brake with the other. The shotgun guard, on his feet, peered ahead, and the whiskered man, sensing danger, moved crablike back across the hurricane with a thought of escaping over the side, but a voice, high-pitched and obviously disguised, came from the blackness of the mountain bank close beside them:

"Hands up!"

The guard froze for half a second, then he tried to come around with his shotgun. From below came a flash and concussion. The guard was hit and knocked backward across the seat. Frightened, the horses tried to bolt. The lead team got itself halfway across a log that the robbers had felled across the road. The driver gee-hawed and cursed and got the other teams stopped short of capsizing the coach down the steep side of the mountain. While this was going on, the guard would have slipped from the seat and fallen between the coach and the horses, but John, without lowering his hands, managed to reach with his legs and catch him, boot toes under the armpits. And he kept holding him that way.

All this had happened very quickly. Now a man came down, on foot, nimble over the rocks, masked by means of a kerchief tied to his hatbrim, his clothes covered by a blanket, a silver-plated gun shining in his right hand.

"Stay een-side!" he warned the passengers.

He disguised his voice, trying to make it sound French, but disguise or not, John knew he had heard that voice before. In Californy, maybe. Or I-de-ho. It gave him a bad feeling. If he knew the fellow, then the fellow likely knew him. And John did not like being known by somebody who had the drop on him. It was a temptation to risk going for his guns. He had a chance, in the dark. On the other hand, that same dark hid him, and his black whiskers and black hat were sort of a disguise. As he thought of those things the man looked right at him and away again, and he was not recognized. He decided to sit tight.

A light had appeared uphill in the timber. Someone carried it down. It was a tin lantern with air vents top and bottom and with a door that opened and closed. Right now, the door was closed.

The French-voiced leader said to stop. The lantern was then around at the rear of the coach. Shadow figures of men commenced moving from the shadows all around. The leader, disguising his voice more heavily than ever, said, "Pass-en-jare, no fear. No rob. Only mail, eek-spress."

John still could not place the voice, but he was more certain than ever.

The thing had been well planned. They already had dragged the express and mail from the rear boot. By light from the can lantern they cut the sacks open and scattered the mail all over the ground. They were looking for one particular thing, and finally it turned up in the form of a large, starched-linen envelope with dabs of wax around the flap.

"That's him," said one of the men, indicating the name with his thumb.

"Open eet!" said the leader.

The man tried, but the stiffened linen was very tough. He drew his bowie, but the leader checked him. "Later," he said, taking the letter and putting it away inside his blanket, and inside his shirt, too, but not before Comanche John, leaning far over, looking directly down, saw the address on the envelope. Unfortunately he had never learned to read and write, so he could not be certain, but recognition jolted him anyway. The lettering was familiar, just as the tracings of a map might be familiar. He had seen those written words time and again when he was with the Parson, and by grab, *yes*—that must be the Parson's name. The letter had been addressed to the Reverend Jeremiah Parker.

Now the leader was ready to leave, but his men were more reluctant.

One of them said, "How about that strongbox?"

"Leave eet."

"Why the hell leave it? It's no more trouble to—"

"Leave eet!" And he added, "Ordairs!"

The lantern had been extinguished. The holdup men quickly faded into the shadows. With a ring and clatter of hoofs on rock, they were gone, riding swiftly away down the stage road, and the passengers, who up till then had been almost silent, started shouting all at the same time.

"It's the Crow Rock Gang," one of them said. And another: "The Crow Rock nothing, they don't get *this* far from Idaho, that was Dutch Hymie and Little Bob," but the driver quieted them all.

"No, it warn't the Crow Rock gang and it warn't Dutch and Bob, neither. What do you back-Easterners know about holdup men, anyhow? You see that one yonder in the black hat? The way he stood there, spread-legged! And the way he held those Navies! Tell you there's only *one man* in all the West holds his Navies like that, and that's the rippingest, rearingest, shootingest ya-hoo that ever come up the long trail from Californy. Yes, gents, he was nobody else than the one and only Comanche John!"

CHAPTER TWELVE

THE TIMBER was lifted out of the road, the mail stuffed back inside its damaged sacks, and Comanche John got the guard lying as best he could on the hurricane. He bandaged him, too, chewing tobacco and sticking it over his side wound, doing it under a considerable handicap, because by that time the coach was rolling, and the driver singing in a voice that reached the far limestone cliffs of the mountain and bounded back again.

> *"Oh, halter up your pony*
> *And listen unto me,*
> *Whilst I sing of old Comanche John,*
> *The fastest gun thar be;*
> *He was born back in Missouri,*
> *In a county name of Pike,*
> *And whenever he draws his twin Nav-ees*
> *'Tis share and share alike.*
>
> *"He had a pal named Jimmy Dale*
> *And one called Dirty Bob—"*

The guard grimaced from pain and whispered to Comanche John, "Make him quit it. Ain't it enough to be shot by that low, bushwhackin' varmint without a drunken coach driver singing what a hell of a fellow he is?"

"Warn't the Comanche shot you. I guarantee it."

They rolled to the bottom, crossed a creek almost belly-deep on the horses, and halted at a stage station. This was Sulphurwater, still fourteen miles from New Boston.

They carried the guard inside a cabin and put him to bed. John stood outside, thinking that he had no hankering to ride into camp atop a newly robbed coach. What he would really like was get hold of that envelope, and with a horse and plenty of luck he just might do it.

He walked among the freight wagons, having a look at the saddle stock. Five minutes later he had made a dicker, buying a cayuse pony and a Pennsylvania pancake saddle for the last three ounces of gold left from his Apex medicine business of the January before.

A half-breed roustabout set him on a cut-across trail to Shauvegan Gulch where New Boston lay. He set out at a gallop, taking the edge off his mean little pony, and settled down to a trot, first following the creek trail, then turning off at the second fork and climbing to the crest of a low ridge.

A rolling, grassy country lay ahead of him, its gentle contours brought out by the highlights and deep shadows of moonlight. The deep mark closest him was Shauvegan Gulch. New Boston, he judged, was well toward its mouth, almost directly west. He could see a light or two. Over the next ridge lay the White Pine, the main creek of the area, in whose valley the Parson and his emigrants had settled, taking up quarters, he supposed, in the old fur-company buildings.

He rode to the gulch. There was no placering there; the gold was all farther down, where some little side streams entered. He kept riding until, on reaching a little round-topped hill, he had a fine view of the gulch for half a mile in both directions; there he freshened his chaw, and waited.

A voice came over the distance, and another answered. He watched. Riders were briefly in view along the gulch rim, before dropping from sight. They were too far to overtake. He cursed, but not vehemently. One against eight or nine—it would be a poor gamble anyway.

He rode, taking his easy time, following the gulch, keeping watch for prospect holes, and was at the outskirt shanties and wickiups of New Boston about midnight.

It was more of a town than he had expected—a thousand, even two thousand people, only months old but already boasting a cluster of two-story buildings, one of them with a stone front. The camp seemed to be busy, but with no particular excitement. The stage probably had not arrived yet, and as he had no desire to be around when it did, he rode on, across placer trenches, around the tail end of a large sluice, under a flume that dripped water on him, over a gentle, sparsely wooded ridge toward the White Pine.

Dawn grew up around the horizon, just gray, still no touch of yellow or red as he rode down on the log buildings and stockade of the old fur post where the Parson's emigrants had settled.

A dog barked at him. It was that mangy black-and-tan hound of Stott's. A woman had just kindled a fire under an outside kettle to heat wash water. She stood watching him as he rode through the open gate. The woman was Mrs. Dilworth. Recognizing him, she opened her mouth to speak, but no sound came. She was scared, and he guessed what the reason was.

"Sister Dilworth, I'm here in the flesh, and if you've heard any rumors of me being hung over in I-de-ho City, put 'em down to brag talk by vigilantes." He dismounted, staying clear of the pony's head for fear of being bitten. "Be the Parson hyar?"

She directed him to the Parson's hut, one of a long line of shanties all with a common roof. He opened the door and spoke into the dark interior.

"Parson, be ye thar? It's Comanche John."

"John, John!" the Parson cried, startled from sleep. "John, let me feel of you." He came barefoot, groping, and felt him up and down. "Yes, it *is*. Oh, blessed day! I read in the Salt Lake paper that they'd hung ye dead down in Idaho City."

"Yes, and tomorrow ye'll hear that I robbed the New Boston coach."

"John, ye didn't! Ye haven't gone back to your old ways of wretchedness!"

"Don't worry about me, Parson. I ain't no fair-weather Christian. I ridden the trail of rectitude, been an honest miner, tried my hand at doctoring, was a success, too, only I lost my best patient. Through no fault o' mine. Believe me, Parson, I haven't lightened a coach since I-de-ho, but I *would have* last night if I'd known." And he told about the envelope, addressed, he was certain, to the Reverend.

Exuberance left the Parson. "Yes," he said, "I just knew something would happen to it."

He struck sparks on tinder, blew flame, and carried it to a candle. He could have opened the door for light, but he preferred it this way because of the early cold. He kept up a steady shivering. His legs, protruding from the woolsey nightshirt, seemed to be all tendons and bone. His head he carried tilted to one side, bent that way by the blow Hames had given him before on Big Hole Pass.

"Ye know what the letter was, then?"

"Alas," said the Parson, "I do."

His resigned attitude annoyed Comanche John, who spat tobacco juice at the cold ashes of a little fireplace and said, "Waal, don't give me any of that 'Lord giveth and Lord taketh away' because it don't count with things like letters. War it important?"

"I'll tell you how important it is—without it we'll probably get run right off'n this ground," the Parson said, showing more life. "I been *waiting* for that letter. It was the original grant made to the Western Fur Company in 1846. Signed by James K. Polk, President of the United States."

"War he Union or Confederate?"

"What difference does that make? The point is, that paper is the only title to this valley that we have. Without that the whole thing falls under mining-district law—hay fields, potatoes, everything, even this house we're standing in. It'll go to the first man to build corner posts and sink to bedrock. Fact is, they were doing it already."

"You mean there's gold here?"

"I don't know. I suppose, maybe."

In exasperation John asked, "Well, why don't *you* fellows stake it?"

"We're not miners, we're farmers." Then the Parson added, "Well, we *did* sink some shafts but we couldn't get to bedrock. Too much groundwater. You know how deep bedrock is? Thirty-five to fifty feet."

"How ye know if ye didn't get to it?"

"Kippen witched for it."

"Oh, I put no stock in them forked sticks."

"Me, either. But this wasn't a forked stick. This is some broomstraw tied in the middle with hair. He holds it by just one hair, a different hair depending on which thing he's looking for, and the way it goes bobbing and weaving, just like it was alive—"

"Parson, I'm surprised at you. That straw is probably off'n a witch's broom, tied with some of her own hair. Or the devil's. I'd look at that hair and see if it warn't singed at the ends. By the way, has he tried it out on gold? If that's the devil's hair, it should work on gold, because gold is the devil's own metal."

"It don't work on gold. Don't worry, if Kippen had something that worked on gold he'd never lay hand to a plow line again."

Comanche John put little faith in Kippen's witch stick, having seen the failure of too many such things in Californy, but he was inclined to agree that bedrock in the White Pine lay as much as fifty feet deep. It might even lie seventy-five or a hundred—those flat, wide valleys were like that.

He said, "Parson, I doubt you got a thing to fear from the miners. If it's that deep to bedrock and water like ye say, nobody'd be fool enough to try mining it. It's safe for your potatoes."

"I tell you they're staking it already."

"Some men'll stake anything. They'll move off and abandon it."

"Then why are they after the grant that gives us title to it? Answer that. You saw 'em take it yourself. Important enough to rob a coach for. You think *they* want to plant potatoes?"

That stumped Comanche John.

The Parson said, "Besides, it's no stray prospector that staked this ground. Not by a jugful. Hackven, Overfelt, Hoss Noon—that bunch. They're the ones tried to stake it."

"*Tried?*"

"Well, yes," the Parson admitted reluctantly. "To tell the truth there was some shooting, and we run 'em off."

"I heared of Hackven," John said, his eyes narrowed, thinking far back. "He was run out of Mackay Bar for claim jumping. And Hoss Noon—it seems to me I've heared of him, too."

"Oh, it wasn't *them*. I mean, not just them. They're saloon toughs. Too lazy to mine. They were sent here. There's somebody behind 'em. Somebody out of sight, telling 'em what to do."

"Hames?"

The Parson had almost forgotten there was a man named Hames, he had had so much trouble since the autumn before. "Oh, him. He's somewhere else, over yonder, across the pass. He's honest now. In the freight business. Hear he's bought part interest in a coach line. No, somebody else. *Who*, I don't know. That's a fact, I don't. I don't know who it is, nor what he wants of the White Pine. Of course, there's Judge Harrison. He's United Sates Commissioner. *Calls* himself that, anyhow. Calls himself U. S. marshal. He's in it, too. Only he's no better'n Hackven and those saloon toughs. I'm worried, John. Worried sick. That Harrison will try to put us off the ground, now that the grant is lost."

"If I were you," said John, "I wouldn't worry too much, because the more I think of it, the more it seems to me I ought to pay a visit to New Boston, yonder, and get that paper back."

"John, could ye? Could ye?" He clutched the sleeve of John's shirt in pleading. "Oh, John, I'd bless ye if ye could. I'm getting near the end of my rope, John—"

"Road agents git to the ends of ropes," said John sourly. "Preachers turn over the last pages of their books."

"All right, anyhow I am. The twilight of my years has come. I'm weary and bowed with care."

"You're tough as bull jerky. You'll outlive me and my horse both. But I'll do it. Damnation, I will. I swore I lifted my hand the last time for these punkin-rollers of yours, but I'll do it."

Through the cabin's tiny window he glimpsed the Widow Cobb. "Parson," he whispered, "be there a back door out o' hyar?"

"What's got into you?" asked the Parson, alarmed. "What did you see? Are the vigilantes after you again?"

"Not after me. I taught them vigilantes a lesson they're not likely to forget."

"Oh," he said, seeing over John's shoulder. "It's Sister Cobb. I thought you got along mighty well with Sister Cobb."

"Parson, I git along too well with her."

"She'd make a good wife for a man. She'd knit and she'd mend. She'd keep the fire burning under the stew pot."

Yes, thought John, *she would.* She made an uncommon good venison stew, both the dumpling kind and the brown-gravy kind. By grab, John had never put mouth anywhere else to the kind of a stew the widow made. And she had promised to knit him a pair of genuine, old-time, natural gray, longhair wool and hair socks, with the soft wool inside and the long guardhair out, the kind a man could put on and keep on all winter, not getting out of once, and have 'em get warmer all the time.

"Yes, but she don't only want to marry me, she wants to *bury* me. Now amongst the Blackfeet it's different. When a Blackfoot gal's husband dies she don't go around with plumes having a big time for herself. She pulls all her hair out by the roots, and then she covers her head with wet-up ashes which she *leaves* there, and she wails day and night until the moon changes, and sometimes she starves to death. Widowhood, Parson, ain't something that a *Blackfoot* gal looks forward to."

CHAPTER THIRTEEN

COMANCHE JOHN rode back to New Boston through the bright noon sun. He kept thinking about Hackven, trying to remember what he looked like, what he *sounded* like, wondering if his was that familiar voice he had heard the night before. No, he got to thinking, that fellow wasn't Hackven. Hackven, if he was recollecting the right man, was taller, and he had a whisky-hoarse voice.

He thought he would recognize Hackven if he met him, and probably Hackven would recognize *him*. Lots of people might recognize him. Best he disguise himself. With this thought, he visited a Chinese barber who trimmed his hair and shaved his cheeks, leaving his black whiskers at a neat point, banker style. He did not look like a banker, though. He looked like an old woolly wolf who had just visited a barber. He walked down the corduroy sidewalk, past all manner of saloons and dives, feeling naked with the air cold on his shorn face, and stopped at a saloon called the Grizzly Bear.

It was a good name. The Parson had mentioned it as the roughest in camp, and hangout for Hackven and his crowd. Nobody looking like them was there now. The bartender, a medium big, mean-looking man with a Wells Fargo gun in a shoulder holster, was behind the deserted bar, fanning flies away, trying to sleep while standing. A faro game moved listlessly. Four miners and a down-at-the-heel gambler in greenish serge and a Louisiana planter's hat played poker for stakes so small the house was not even raking off the game.

The bartender and the faro dealer both stirred hopefully when John entered, but they settled back again when he slouched to the rear, fetched a chair for himself, and tilted it against the rear wall.

The afternoon passed. John rested. He chawed and spat at a distant sawdust box that served as a spittoon. It grew dark in the long, almost windowless room, and with the sun still up, a Negro man lit several lights.

"Big cleanup today at the Nugget," he remarked, referring to one of the camp's most productive placer mines.

The faro dealer said he hoped so because he hadn't seen anything bigger than a white chip all day.

At that moment, three men came inside, whooping and jostling one another. One of them dumped a quantity of gold dust on the bar, asked that it be weighed, then the three of them commenced drinking it up, talking about guns, horses, and squaws.

John sat on the hind legs of his chair thinking how nine-tenths of all saloon talk was about guns, horses, and squaws. Chiefly squaws.

One of these fellows, a filthy, powerful, large-mouthed man, was loudly allowing how one time, a year or two back, when he was hauling government freight, he'd had every squaw between Lewiston and Walla Walla running from him. Yes, he had. It used to be that his outfit had only to come in sight, a mile or two away, and you should see those Injuns break camp, pull up their tepees, hide their women, both young and old, and run for the bushes.

"That sounds a bit farfetched to me, Hoss," said a tall, loose-jawed man with a drooping yellow mustache. "Lately you ain't even been able to make up to that squaw of Tolbert's."

John took new notice. These were his men. The dirty one was Hoss Noon, and that tall one was Hackven. Yes, of course he was Hackven. Only he'd grown that long yellow mustache, and stained the underside of it brown with tobacco, since John last saw him. The one he heard called "Clip," so he was Clip Overfelt. Then, a few minutes later, two others arrived, one of them a small, wiry man with what looked like a club-foot, the other very broad and muscular, built not un-like John himself, and carrying his pistols in John's manner, too. That one proved to be Missou. Missou, he thought, had been the one with the lantern. The limping one, Billy Step-and-a-Half, had been there, too. Of course, *all* of them had been there. Only as yet there was no sign of their leader, the one with the French accent.

Now was his time, John decided, so he let his chair thump forward, got up, yawned and stretched, and ambled to the bar.

"Whisky!" he said.

The bartender was too busy refereeing a dice game between Hoss and Missou to pay attention to him. John struck the bar with the heel of his fist and roared, "Whisky, or would ye rather I parted your hair with a thirty-six-caliber comb?"

That brought the bartender around. He stepped back and looked at John without favor. The dice game stopped. Everybody looked at him. The bartender said, "So you did come to life, after all. I'd about de-cided you thought this was a hotel. And now all of a sudden after wearing out the hind legs of that expen-sive chair, freighted here all the way from Salt Lake, you want a lot of quick service."

"I divide my time into halves," John said. "Daytime is my sleeping half, and nighttime is my drinking half."

The bartender set out an empty glass and batted it down the bar with a contemptuous back of the hand. He hooked a jug of trade whisky and slid *that* down the bar.

"Not that," said Comanche John. "I drink nothing but the best." His eyes were on a fancy decanter of Old Haversill Bourbon that occupied the place of honor on the backbar, a showpiece, intended not for drinking but for style. *"That."*

The bartender couldn't believe his ears. "That?" he asked, pointing instead to a half-gone bottle of cheaper whisky.

"No," said John. He moved a step toward the middle of the room; his right shoulder dipped, and there was a backward slouch of his body. A Navy exploded with a finger of powder flame over the edge of the bar and the fancy bottle of Old Haversill stood neckless with bits of glass and cork zinging the air.

"That!"

The explosion had stopped all other sounds in the room. As everyone stared, Comanche John chawed and spat and reholstered his Navy.

"Gittin' so's a Californy man can't make himself understood speakin' the English lang'age. Country full up with abolitionists, draft dodgers, and Illini farm boys. Don't understand the English lang'age. Got to teach 'em. That's what a man's got to do. He's got to teach 'em."

With awed deference the bartender set down the decapitated bottle of Old Haversill, and John poured from its shattered neck. "Messy job," he complained, looking at the jagged glass. "Putting no glass in the bottles these days. Cheapness showing up everywhere. Time was that a bullet would nick off a bottle clean as an undertaker's chin, but no more, no more."

"Say!" cried Missou after holding his breath a long ten seconds. "That was *shootin'!*"

"Oh, it warn't bad for home-cast bullet and ordinary Pennsylvania powder. You can't tell it, seeing the bottle is broke, but I wouldn't be surprised if that bullet was as much as a quarter of an inch off. Now for real fine shooting, like, say, I was to shoot that fly off the bartender's ear—"

"Never you mind," said the bartender, shooing the fly away himself. "You did enough damage. You ruint that bottle, and you'll have to pay for the whole thing of it."

"As I was saying," John went on, "it might be a fourth off. Now if I had a machine-polished bullet, and German powder, *weighed*, mind ye, not measured, *then* I'd be in position to show ye some real shooting."

Hackven said, "You're not that Captain What's-His-Name that's billed for the Montana House?"

"I'm no stage shooter. I'm not generally even a bottle shooter."

Missou yipped in appreciation. "You mean you're a man shooter!"

"Well," John was bound to admit, "I have rid the country of a few snakes."

"*This* country?"

"More like I-de-ho country, and Californy country."

"I seen you some place before," said Hackven.

John looked him cold in the eye. "I doubt it. I never seen you before. None of you."

Hackven shrugged. "All right, if that's how you want it!"

"That's how I want it. Now, for instance, say some day ye was to see a picture that looked like me on a ree-ward poster. It ain't me. It's some other fellow. It's Jimmy Dale, or Three-Gun Bob, or that poor, departed Comanche John, the greatest of them all, who this evenin' lies cold and dank in his grave, hung by vigilantes down in I-de-ho City."

"Have it your way. How you making a living? Mining?"

John looked at his hands—strong hands, rather stub-fingered, but not a callus on them.

"I'd rate me as more like a skilled craftsman."

Hackven knew what he meant. "And so you came here. What did you have told you that you looked us up?"

"I heared ye was—well, craftsmen."

"Who told you?"

"Word gets around. Maybe, for instance, I war told by somebody right in this room."

The boys moved uncomfortably and looked at one another.

"We could use him," said Missou.

"Keep quiet," said Hackven. "I'll tell you all in due time whether we can use him or not."

But Missou gave John a wink, and he knew that things were all right.

Comanche John drank with them, taking less than he seemed to, listening for stray bits of information. The evening ended in a brawl, with Missou and Overfelt fighting Turk-fashion, each with his hands in his pockets, teeth clamped to opposite ends of an old shirt, first to let go or take his hands from his pockets being the loser. Actually it was a head-knocking contest at which Missou won.

After the contest, Overfelt lay bleeding on the floor and no amount of whisky would revive him.

Finally Hackven said, "Quit pouring that likker into him. He's just drunk, that's all that's wrong with him. You want to revive him, you better throw him in the crick."

This was done, and it worked, after a manner; at least Overfelt was able to walk with one man's help, but by then the boys were making the town and they lost him somewhere along the way.

John slept in a shack with Hoss Noon, Missou, Hackven, and Billy Step-and-a-Half. At dawn, the hour when he arose, winter and summer, they were still sprawled on the floor, snoring, so he pulled on his boots and stepped over them, going to the door.

Hackven awoke, saw who it was, grimaced from the pain of light striking his eyes, and said, "Anything you heard last night keep to yourself, understand?"

"You don't need to give me those orders."

"Well, they're gave. I got nothing against you, Smith. Fact is, I feel sort of cut from your cloth. Both old Californy men, and all. So you take it on the quiet side. If your poke is a little bit light, maybe you'll get a chance to put some of the heavy color into it. I don't guarantee it, but I'll see."

"Thankee." John knew better than ask *who* he would see.

"And one other thing," Hackven said, sitting up again. "You going yonder for grub?" he meant to the town. "Well, you stay clear of the Montana House. None of our men hang around the Montana House." He lay down and sat up yet again to call to John outside the door. "And don't ask why!"

John walked down the crooked gulch street looking across the roofs of lesser buildings at the fancy frame cornices of the Montana House. The building was mostly of logs, but those cornices must have been brought in all the way from Missouri, or from one of the new mills in Seattle, and they did give the building a touch of class.

He ate at a beanery, a log-sided building with a canvas roof, paying over a fifth-ounce of gold for a meal worth no more than half of that. Everything in New Boston was high—except for whisky. That season, so many freighters had gone in for barrel cargoes that whisky was selling cheaper than in Walla Walla, even.

"Three-dollar-fifty is a mighty high price for two eggs and one bitty boiled potato," he complained, hefting the meager lump of dust left in the bottom of his poke.

The proprietor, who had worked all night and was surly, answered, "Looks to me like you got a bargain considering the pale-looking dust you paid off with. This dust never came from Shauvegan Gulch, nor the Chiny diggings, either. Dilute my whole cash drawer with this sort of dust. Git any more customers like you and the bank will commence raising my brassage, and there my profits will go, right down the crick."

At the door to go outside John said, "That gold ain't a damn bit paler than your coffee."

The restaurant man was saying to himself, "Raise my brassage, will they? They got the last ounce of color off me. I'm selling to *Hames* from here on."

The name stopped John and made him come back. "Who?"

"Hames."

"Lawford?"

"Why, the same Hames that was Pelton and Hames down in Coloraydo, only Pelton passed away. You know him?"

"What made ye think I knew him?"

"You called him Lawford."

"Oh, so I did. It might be I do. I known a plenty of people up along the trail. He running the Montana House?"

"No, Malloy runs the Montana House. I don't know where Hames is. I never saw the fellow, even. He's got a coach running in here, competition to the Utah and Northern. Gold-buying agency, express. Insures everything. New York outfit, insurance. Surety Forwarding and Sight Draft, something like that. Hames is agent. He don't own the insurance company, only the coach. Insurance, though! That's what the country needs."

"Hames, eh?"

"Really first class."

"That's Hames for a certainty, really first class." He walked on muttering to himself. Damned if ye didn't have to admire a man like Hames, how he could pull himself up by his own bootstraps. Say! That was a clever way of putting it. John wondered if he'd made that up himself or if he'd heard it some place—pulling himself up by his own bootstraps.

He spent the day loafing in one place and another, chiefly in the Grizzly Bear Saloon. Missou showed up looking pouchy and mean, complaining about the Shauvegan Gulch drinking water which was bad for his system, giving him indigestion. Headache, too. Pain right behind his eyeballs. Then Hoss came around and reminded Missou of the *temperance meeting* they were supposed to attend, and that was the last John saw of them until late that night when he was awakened at the shanty.

He sat up, Navy in hand, and said, "Ho, thar!"

"It's us," said Missou. "Go back to sleep."

"Ask him now," said the voice of Hoss Noon from the blackness.

Hackven said, "I'll ask him. You complain of a light poke, Smith. Maybe you'd like to weighten it up a little."

"I would," said John. "I would for a certainty."

"Tomorrow, then."

"Coach too heavy-loaded?"

"Say," said Hoss, "that's putting it pretty good. Coach too heavy-loaded. Lighten it up. Gold's heavy. Heaviest thing there is."

"Coach, eh?" said John.

"Maybe," said Hackven. "You'll find out."

"Which coach is it?" Comanche John was willing to bet the last color in his poke it would be a Utah & Northern coach, the outfit Hames was competing with.

"Never you mind. It'll be easy, that I guarantee. Quite a favor we're doing you, Smith. A chance to ride up and fill your poke. No danger, even."

"Ain't a man entitled to *some* details?"

"You're filling your purse. That's details enough. You're getting as many details as I give anybody else."

After the others were snoring, Missou rolled close to Comanche John and whispered, "Hackven's showing off. *He* don't know what coach it is himself. He won't know until tomorrow, just before we ride."

"Until he visits the Montana House?"

"Until that drunken *old Judge Harrison* visits the Montana House."

Comanche John was wrong about it being a Utah & Northern coach. It proved to be Hames's coach. Easy job. The shotgun guard had been taken ill, a fat consumption-and-asthma-cure salesman sat in his place on the high seat, and the box of cast bullion bars of gold were where Hackven knew they would be, inside a secret compartment behind the rear seat. John wanted one of the bullion bars as his share right then, but Hackven said, "Later on."

Two days later, in New Boston, John got as his split a poke of gold, regular Chiny Gulch dust, the bullion having been disposed of he knew not how.

Again there was nothing to do but take his ease in one saloon or another. He learned nothing about the Parson's grant. The Montana House remained forbidden ground. The gang was not to be seen loitering there. So one evening, there he was, in the Montana, a theater, bar, and gambling house, probably the largest in the territory.

He played faro. In the theater, an orchestra consisting of a cornet, a violin, and a harp commenced to play. The theater offered standing room and some boxes with painted-screen fronts where the new-rich tycoons of Chiny Gulch and the Shauvegan could drink champagne with their women friends and see without being seen.

On a tiny, gilt-arched stage the show commenced. It was a rowdy show presenting the same performers over and over in songs, dances, and comic dialogues. Then: "The feature attraction of the evening, direct from St. Louis, Noo Yawk, and Paris, France, the Songbird of the Seine, Mademoiselle Louise Deveroux, *La Belle Gants de Soie.*"

Mademoiselle proved to be on the large side, but well-curved, buxom, brunette, and beautiful. She wore a white gown covered with spangles, and lace gloves to her elbows. In mid-stage she waited until the crowd quieted, then posturing, clasping her hands, with a French accent forgotten after first measure, she sang "A Handful of Earth from Molly's Grave."

But this was only the start. She had introduced that song for class. Now, in response to cheers and suggestions from the boot-stomping audience, she let out a little, tremulous war cry, pulled off her dress, and left herself seductive and agleam in cream-colored tights with spangles.

"Hoo-raw!" shouted Comanche John as she pranced around, singing a rowdy river song. "Hoo-raw for *La Belle Gants de Soie!*"

Comanche John got so close that his whiskers, which were now growing to something like their previous abundance, were singed in the flames of the footlights. He was so close he could smell the perfume she wore. She was the most beautiful woman he had ever seen, and the best scented. At the conclusion of her number he threw gold nuggets from his purse until she had to take notice of him.

"Would ye do me the honor?" asked John, bowing with black slouch hat in hand and one jackboot thrust forward, waving toward one of the gilded boxes.

"Ah, *oui!*" she cried. "I dreenk champagne."

"Champagne!" roared Comanche John from the box, striking the spindly table with fist and forearm.

A Chinese boy must have been awaiting just those words. In he popped through the door at the back with the bottle and two glasses.

"You would like female amusement?" he asked.

"Just leave that bottle; I'm *gittin'* female amusement."

Comanche John opened the bottle by knocking its neck off with his navy. The champagne was warm and wild. He drank the top two inches to save it. It got all bubbly up his nose.

He heard someone at the door. He thought it was La Belle. He stood up and again swept off his black slouch hat. But it was not La Belle. Standing, facing him, was Sanchez—Sanchez the barber—Sanchez whom last he had seen helping Hames with his dirty work over on the I-de-ho side.

It was a surprise to both of them.

"I should kill ye," said John. "I should for old times' sake. Ye got it coming, and that's a fact. What the hell are ye doing here?"

Sanchez recovered himself and showed his yellowish teeth in a smile. "Oh, here I am what you call bouncer."

This was the voice. His was the *French* accent of Moosehorn Pass. A Mexican, pretending to be French, talking English—no wonder he hadn't recognized it.

"You mean you've come to bounce me?"

"Well, you know, in a polite way. The boss, he says no road agents."

"Then what are *you* doing here?"

"Well, none of Hackven's gang, except on the quiet, back way, *sabe?* Of course, if it was me, you, my friend, amigo—"

"No, I ain't your friend. I have no part of renegades who toss in with Injuns, massacre wagon trains."

"Nor *me!* Did I not queet that man so soon as I learned? Believe me, señor, I am an honest barber. Oh, how I would like to shave the throat of that man Hames after the way he hoodweenked me. So close I would shave him, all the way down to his weendpipe. But tonight—"

"I hope you got no thought of telling anybody who I be."

"Smith. I remember. The name is Smith."

"Smith. You tell anybody that I'm Comanche John I'll come gunning for ye. Or if ye get me arrested. You do, Sanchez, and I'll tell 'em all of that deal yonder. The Big Hole. I'll not only do that, I'll get witnesses over here, honest farmers, plenty of 'em."

"I know. They have worried me a great deal."

"You wish they'd leave the country?" John asked, his eyes narrowing.

He shrugged, guessing he had said too much.

"How about Hames? Does *he* wish they'd leave the country!"

"That dog, that swine, son of a peeg fathered by a burro."

"Whar's that land grant?" John asked, trying to catch him off guard.

"Eh?"

"You know! Whar is that government grant to the White Pine, the one you and your boys robbed off that coach on Moosehorn Pass?"

His eyes narrowed. "You weesh it?"

"Yes."

"A deal, señor." He looked both ways and tried to come close, but John was too wary for that, and kept him beyond the table. "A bargain. I will get the paper for you; you will forget about the Big Hole, the Indians, everything."

"When?"

"Tomorrow. Next week for sure. I must go very carefully. You wait. Do nothing. And from this building—*get out*."

CHAPTER FOURTEEN

COMANCHE JOHN did not get out. He sat with his jackboots on the table and waited for La Belle. What he should have done, he thought, was shoot Sanchez the second he pushed the door open. That would have been the safe way. There was no trusting Sanchez. One thing was certain, though—Sanchez was scared of those Pikes Peakers. Good reason, too. They were always a danger, living so close. There was always a chance of them stirring up trouble about that Big Hole business. Folks here in the Nor'west had plenty of toleration; they overlooked killing unless it was from behind, and they forgot about robbery given a year or three, but they never got around to tolerating a white man who tossed in with the Injuns to attack a wagon train. It probably explained why Hames went for that grant, too—so he could jump claim in the valley and move the Parson and his crew away to some spot where they wouldn't be so likely to cause him trouble. Hames was getting to be a great man in the territory now; he wouldn't want his past to jump up and bite him.

Comanche drank more champagne. The taste of it gagged him. He had a chaw of tobacco to take the sweet taste of champagne out of his mouth. La Belle did not arrive. He left the box, followed a narrow hall, and wandered the building, getting the lay of the ground. He climbed some narrow, private stairs to the second story. A short, broad, sour-mouthed man with a sawed-off shotgun across his knees awoke with a jump when he felt the floor under Comanche John's weight.

"Oh, you!" said the guard. "You're one of Hackven's men."

"I'm nobody's man. Put that gun down. I don't like cocked guns being pointed at me. I'm here to see your boss."

"Malloy?"

"Yes. And Hames, too."

"I know nothing about any Hames. You must have the wrong place if you're looking for a Hames. But as for Malloy, you ain't seeing him. You ain't supposed to be in this building at all. You get out."

John roared, "Fetch Malloy!"

The guard shouted right back, "Get out!" And with the sawed-off shotgun cocked and aimed, and his finger riding a bit too heavily on the trigger, it was his voice which carried the greater authority.

John had learned which was the door to Malloy's room, anyhow. It was this one, right at hand, the only genuine mahogany door with fancy brass fittings to be found in the whole establishment. Yonder was a rear door, obviously to some outside stairs. To his right was a door leading to a little four-by-four room and a ladder. The ladder, of course, led to a firehole through the roof. As the building was almost square, and Malloy's room about in the middle of it, there would be no outside window. He had noticed some skylights, four of them, when he rode down from the high country a few days back. The firehole, north-northeast, six-seven paces, would mark the correct skylight so he could find it from topside.

"If ye insist on being impolite about it," said John, "why, I'll have to concede to ye. So, I bid ye good night."

Malloy wasn't there or he'd have come out when John shouted. Now was the time. Now was the time, indeed, before Sanchez carried the word around that Smith of the banker's whiskers was really black-bearded Comanche John.

He went around back. There were the outside stairs, as he had surmised. He climbed to the second-story landing, stood on the railing, dug some of the mud chinking from between the logs, got toe and finger grips, and chinned himself over the edge of the roof.

The roof was flat-slanty, with a covering of tar and gravel. There was a slight moon. Light came from one of the four skylights. Not the one above Malloy's room, however. It was open on a prop pole. Standing over it, he could feel a gentle current of warm, rising air from inside the building—air carrying the faint odor of cigar and furniture polish.

"Ho, thar!" he said softly into the opening, just in case someone was below. He got no answer. He opened the skylight full, lowered himself inside, hung swinging his feet around the void, and dropped.

He was in luck. There was a table beneath the skylight, and whereas he had steeled himself against a drop of perhaps six feet, he fell barely eighteen inches.

He lit a sulphur match, lit a lamp, and took time to look around.

The room was luxuriously furnished, compared with most rooms in that country. There was not a puncheon chair around. There were rugs on the floor. On a sideboard were a bottle of Kentucky whisky and a box of rare Cuban cigars.

John had just a nip of the whisky and lit one of the cigars and, thus made comfortable, proceeded quietly to search the room, taking everything out and putting it back again. He took his time, he was half an hour at it, but he failed to find the government grant.

He cursed a little, filled his pockets with cigars, blew out the lamp, and got back to the skylight by means of a chair placed on the table. Hanging, he lifted the chair between his feet and dropped it to the floor. Then he chinned himself back to the roof, and outside, rested on one knee to catch his breath.

He realized with a sudden jolt of alarm that someone had moved in the deep shadow right beside him. He started to rise and turn and go for his Navies all at the same instant, and he stopped all of those movements half completed. A gun's cold, hard muzzle was pressed against the back of his neck.

"Git your hands up!" The voice belonged to Hackven. "Yes, Smith, don't you try anything, because I know you now for a double-dealer, and it'd be my supreme pleasure to kill you."

There were other men. Men moved from the shadows of chimneys and of skylights—Clip Overfelt and Hoss Noon and limping Billy Step-and-a-Half.

"Walk!" said Hackven. "Don't try anything—walk!"

Overfelt said, "Aren't you taking his guns?"

"Hell with 'em. I hope he draws. I only *hope* it!"

"Take his guns!"

"You take 'em."

John said, "Lemme unbuckle 'em."

"Keep your hands clear!" Overfelt, careful not to come in front of Hackven, stepped in gingerly and plucked the Navies from the holsters.

Under the muzzle of Hackven's gun, John descended through the firehole. There were more men in the hall below. One was Sanchez; another was a short, stocky fellow wearing a deputy's badge.

"Really got the militia out to take the old Comanche!" John said.

"Walk," said Hackven behind him, prodding him. "Keep walking."

"Whar?"

"You know, the office. Don't try anything. It'd do me good to pull this trigger. We cut you in, easy money, charity almost, and you, you—"

"You talk too much!" said Sanchez. He was thinking about the deputy.

No more was said. Sanchez opened the door to Malloy's office. There sat Malloy, a tall, pale man of thirty, well dressed, nervous-eyed.

"Come on in!" he said tensely.

John did so. He chawed and spat at the spittoon, missing it. That might have indicated a slight nervousness, or it could have been an intended indignity for the rug. He did not look around, but he could feel a gun prodding him.

"What were you looking for?" Malloy asked.

"That's easy enough—my share of the gold."

"You got your share."

"That bitty poke of dust? I figured up my share, my *fair* share, and it comes to exactly three and one-fourth bricks of that bullion."

"You're a liar."

"Say, I don't allow—"

"You weren't after bullion at all."

He knows, thought John. *He knows I was after the grant.*

Malloy was talking again. "Who sent you here?"

"Nobody."

"You're in with the banking company's detectives now, aren't you?" He stood up. "Aren't you?"

Now what kind of crazy idee is that? thought John, but he did not say it. He wanted to hear more.

"Or was it the insurance company?"

John remembered the restaurant man, the one who charged a fifth-ounce for two bitty eggs and one boiled potato, and how he talked about Hames insuring all gold shipments. John had helped rob a Hames shipment; the bullion had come from a secret compartment; Hackven knew very well it was there, and how much would be there. So Hames was robbing himself, letting the insurance company pay his shippers, thus ending with the bullion while making a real honest-John hero of himself.

"Answer me," said Malloy. "The insurance company sent you, didn't they?"

"It could be they did." John chawed. "And it could

be they'll be here with a whole passel of U.S. marshals iffen I should disappear like being shot in the back. So my advice to you is pay over that bullion, all of it, every ounce of it, and that grant to White Pine Valley, too, or *all* of you will end up in an iron-grated house where none o' the hinges work."

A man had stood up. Someone behind him, someone he had not realized was in the room. He had the briefest warning of a blow. Not time to move, even to flinch—it hit like explosion, mixed with blackness in his brain, and the next he knew he was on the floor, arms instinctively wrapped around his head.

He rolled over. His ears rang and he could not see. He was a few seconds like that. Then his eyes focused and he saw Lawford Hames standing over him with a gun in his hand.

John whispered, "So it's the bushwhack king himself!"

Hames smiled with his teeth. He had a tall, triumphant swagger. He stood with his California beaver hat on the back of his head, handsome and knowing it.

"No, *you* weren't sent by any insurance company," he said. "What you were looking for was *this*."

John did not look to see. He knew without looking. He sat holding his head. There was a slick spot on his hair where the gun had cut him. He rubbed his head and the salt of his sweaty hair made it burn like fire.

"That paper will do you no good," said John. "It's made out to *them*. You try forgery on that—"

"So it is. Made out to them." He walked to the lamp, lit the paper, and stood letting it burn in his fingers. "And now there's no grant. Nothing. They got no claim to anything. It's mining district. *As of now* those farmers are trespassing on another man's ground."

"You're a mighty big man, Hames, big-time frieght operator, coach operator. What the hell do ye need of a few acres of creek bottom rightfully belonging to a rag-tag bunch of sodbusters?"

"Nobody double-crosses *me*. Not them, not you. Nobody calls me a renegade. *Them* I'll go easy on. *Them*

I'll give a few hundred dollars to get their wagons rawhided together to pull out of the country. You— well, you're leaving the country, too. With a rope around your neck. Legal. A decision of our Judge Harrison."

"What's the charge?"

"You're the charge! Your own identity. Comanche John!"

"It might amuse ye to know that Comanche John was hung in I-de-ho City within the six months, and hanging the same man twice violates that portion of the legal code known as double jeprody."

Hames laughed at him. "Well, you sell that to the judge." He walked the room, bestrode it, straight, powerful legs filling his fine, kerseymere trousers. His success of the past months had done things for him. He'd really moved up in the world, John was thinking. Well, this was the country a man could do it in—a brand new country plated with gold.

"Yes, convince the judge. Draw up a brief."

"I don't read nor write, as you know, but—"

"And the funniest thing— Listen, Malloy. Here's the funniest thing about it. Do you know where I'll get the money to pay those rotten farmers' way out of the country? Out of my pocket? No. Reward. Reward for Comanche John. Five hundred dollars from Denver City, fifty ounces of gold from the Yellowjacket Union Club, a thousand from the Placer City Express Company. Probably more, too, if we look around."

"*Probably* more?" John said, lifting his head. "Why, that's small no-account money compared with some rewards offered for me. Down in Californy I know about one ree-ward of *ten thousand dollar!*"

With a flourish, Hames took a pencil from his pocket and asked, "Whom do I address?"

"The devil with ye!"

A heavy man was stamping up the stairs, puffing, talking between puffs: "There, there, your arm, sir. Much obliged. Much obliged, indeed. Now, where is the prisoner? Isn't the sheriff here? What the devil is this? Forcing me to climb these steps? They know where my chambers are located."

"There's the judge," said Malloy.

"His old battle wound is really bothering him to-night," said Hames, and they both laughed.

Judge Harrison made it to the door. He stood, leaning against it, getting his breath. He was large, soft, very red of face, about fifty. He wore black serge, stained by food, drink, and cigar ash all down the front. He wore no collar or tie, but his filthy white shirt was held together at the neck by a brass collar button set with a sensational glass ruby. In his hand he carried a rolled-up umbrella. There had been no rain for weeks—the umbrella was for style.

He belched, wheezed, and said, "A pain in my side, gentlemen! These infernal stairs. If you knew what I suffer. An old battle wound, you know. The war for Texas, you know. Is this the prisoner?" he asked, looking at Hackven.

"Meet Comanche John," said Hames.

"Oh, good, good. Say, Comanche John! Well, let us repair to my offices and have the trial. Fair and impartial. The hour is late, but if we hurry we will still have time for the hanging by sunrise."

"It might interest your honor," said John, "to know that Comanche John war already hung in I-de-ho City. Give me one week and I can have the affy-david hyar to prove it."

"Good, good. We'll send for it. Can't take chances, though, you know. We'll hang you on schedule and settle with Idaho City for credit due afterward. I say, is that whisky over yonder?"

A crowd could be heard outside. Word of John's capture had already raced along the streets. In the distance someone was beating a drum.

"What's that?" asked Hames.

Hackven said, "That's Foolish Mike Peabody. His shanty is a mile down the gulch. I wonder how he got wind of it already?"

Foolish Mike was sort of a town crier who went

around beating his drum whenever there was important news, passing the hat for small color. Out of money and lacking other news, Foolish Mike was not above inventing Union or Confederate victories, either of which paid off well from New Boston's partisan populace, but tonight he had real news, and they could hear his hoarse voice accentuated by the boom of the drum: "They caught him, they caught him! *(Boom! Boom!)* Comanche John. *(Boom!)* He'll rob no more; they'll hang him. *(Boom! Boom!)* He robbed the sluice at Whisky Gulch. Killed three men, killed three men. Shot 'em down in co-old blood."

He came booming closer and closer until they could feel the impact of the bass drum from the street below, and there he went on reciting the details of the Whisky Gulch sluice robbery a month before, a foul piece of business in which three miners had been shot from ambush.

John, rolling his head around to get the ache from it, said, "Ain't I guilty of enough without inventing things? I never robbed a sluice in my life. Sluice robbing to my mind is the next lowest thing to slave stealing."

"How about ambush?" asked Hackven. "Some of the stories I hear—"

"Ask Hames about ambush. He's the soo-preme authority."

They tied John's hands behind him, using thongs of rawhide that felt hard as wire. Finch, the deputy, stayed at his back, a gun drawn. Hackven and Noon were on his two sides. Hames stood off by himself, seeing that all was done to his satisfaction, smiling, smoking a cigar, teetering on the toes of his polished boots.

"Coming?" asked Malloy.

"No, I'll stay out of it if you don't mind." He added, knocking the ash off his cigar, "I'll come along tomorrow morning and look at the body."

"Waal, look out it don't rise up and bite ye," said John.

"It won't."

"Bring the guns," Judge Harrison said, reluctantly putting the bottle back. There was only a heel left in it anyhow. "May I recommend Old Stonehouse Bourbon, aged in wood? The guns. No, you fellows aren't getting away with the guns. Evidence. Murder weapons. Prima facie. I can see you don't know much about jurisprudence. Skaggs versus Fitzhugh, year 1783. Do you want them to stalemate us with a writ of habeas corpus?"

"Who?" asked Finch.

"*Them*. Anyone. Those pettifoggers over in Bannock City, I suppose. Damn it, do I have to answer questions from every bailiff? Bring the cigars, too."

"You be careful o' them guns," John said to Hackven. "You git them Navies out o' kilter I'll come around and blast six cubits out o' your middle."

"You'll be dead, and six foot under with your neck stretched out longer'n a whooping crane's. You'll be in condition to do nothing to nobody!"

The rawhide thongs hurt him when he moved. "Mighty tight, mighty painful," he said.

"Mighty dead, the three you bushwhacked at Whisky Gulch," said Deputy Finch.

CHAPTER FIFTEEN

THEY WALKED HIM to the hall, down the stairs. The air was close from the smell of the crowd packed on the floor below. "Make way, make way!" Hoss was saying, shouldering men this way and that. "Don't touch the prisoner."

Men filled the lower rooms, they stood on card tables, they boosted themselves on the bar to get a glimpse of him. "It's him, it's the Comanche!" they were saying. "I seen him in Placerville one time." "Why, I seen *him* around town. *He* the Comanche?" Someone was playing a comb wrapped in paper, stopping at regular intervals to sing in a nasal voice:

> *"Co-man-che came to I-de-ho*
> *With a pal named Injun Ike,*
> *A very shady character*
> *Who was on the jump from Pike;*
> *But Ike got drunk in Lewiston*
> *And ended up in jail,*
> *And they hung him to a cottonwood*
> *Ere John could go his bail."*

"We'll write the last verse of that doggerel tonight," a man whooped.

"There he comes!" someone shouted from the street. "They're bringing the killer now."

"Trial be damned! Give him the same trial he gave the boys at Whisky Gulch."

Someone swung a blow at John as he passed. He weaved, and the blow knocked his hat off. He could not pick it up. His hat was trampled. Someone else picked it up and stuck it back on his head.

"Keep away from the prisoner!" Finch was shouting. "He'll get a fair trial before we hang him. I'll kill any man tries to take my prisoner away from me."

"What you got to say for yourself, killing honest men from ambush?"

John answered, "I say killing them was a typical Yankee trick and I'm for Jeff Davis! I say I warn't even in the country when that was done, and give me a day or two and I can prove it!"

"Listen to him! He wants a day or two! We're supposed to feed him at public expense for *two* days while he proves he ain't where he was."

Some pitch torches burned brightly with large volumes of smoke before the log building that served as a claim recorder's office, judge's office, and jail. He was taken toward it, carried in the sweep of the crowd. Newly sworn deputies were posted to keep clear the front steps of the jail.

Judge Harrison, smelling of freshly consumed liquor, had hurried around by some rear way. He came through his office in time to meet them grandly with a law book under his right arm.

"Trial ready to commence. Where's my gavel? Somebody find my gavel."

"Hold it outside!" everyone started to shout and, acceding to the demand, he had his table carried to the walk.

The platform stood two feet off the ground and made a fair stage. It was cooler there, anyhow. John was thankful for that. A barrel of rainwater stood near the door and he was tempted to dip his head in it, but if he did, it would be like somebody to hold him under. Besides, the water gave him an idea. It was such an idea that he wanted to whoop in glee, but he did not. He stood and looked like a condemned man should look. If only he could get himself *close* to the barrel, and if only it was full enough!

Judge Harrison clubbed the table with his gavel. He did not call a jury. He remarked in a loud voice that there was just time before the trial for the spectators to repair to their favorite bar for a drink of Old Stonehouse Bourbon and started calling the names of witnesses.

He swore in everyone who happened to raise his hand, saying the familiar sentence all in one breath, and then said, "Hoss Noon, take the stand."

Hoss stood and testified that John, when arrested, had two pokes of gold marked with the burned-in initials I.J.R. The two pokes were displayed. John had never seen them before. They were identified as genuine. The gold was identified as the type found in Whisky Gulch. The guns were shown to be .36-caliber like those used in the ambush and, for that matter, like two-thirds of the pistols in camp.

"Evidence conclusive," shouted Harrison. He banged the table with his gavel. "Prisoner guilty. By the power vested in me by the Territorial Legislature and his honor the Governor, all duly elected by the citizens of this territory, I sentence the prisoner to hang by the neck until he is dead; move out o' the way over there so the boys can get the freight wagon up to the mercantile platform, use it for a drop; we'll hang him off the jut-end of the awning."

"Hold on," said John, "can't I speak in my own be-half? What kind of court of law ye running here?"

"Prisoner guilty, no sense in taking up the time of the court." He waved a stubby hand at the gold and John's brace of Navies. "Somebody carry these inside and provide for their safekeeping until such time as proper heirs and assigns have been established. Boy, will you run down to the Montana and fetch me a pint of Old Stonehouse Bourbon, the pride of all Kentucky bourbons aged in the wood?"

As a side line, Judge Harrison was agent for the dis-tillery and never missed an opportunity for advertising his product.

"Dang ye!". cried John. "Give me time to send a let-ter to I-de-ho City and I can prove it's *illegal* to hang me. I can prove I was already hung over in I-de-ho City. Haven't ye ever heared o' double jeprody? What kind of lawyer do ye call yourself anyhow?"

"Prisoner be quiet. Court will fine prisoner for con-tempt."

"I'll tell ye why I'm here," said John. "Not on ac-count of any holdup and ambush at Whisky Gulch or wherever. It's on account of an ambush, right enough, renegade ambush, white men throwing in with Injuns off the Cayuse War, raiding a wagon train, ready to rob white folk, kill 'em if necessary—"

John found himself garroted from behind. Everyone was shouting at once anyhow. No one could hear him. He fought and got free.

"No more of that!" said Finch. "Any more of that, I'll bend a gun barrel over your skull."

"It ain't easy on a man, being hung," John whis-pered, favoring his abused throat, trying a new tack. "Even for a man like me, road agent, gunman wicked enough to shame Gomorrah. No, it ain't. Ain't easy going to face your maker with sin on your soul and your lamp of righteousness nigh run empty. And I got dear ones at home. I don't guess you men of New Boston would want to swing a man without him having a fitten time to pray, and to write to his loved ones."

"Give him time!" some of them started to shout, but others were angrily demanding, "How much time did he give the boys in Whisky Gulch?"

"Gents, all I ask is a minister to help me pray and I'll hang with your praise on my lips."

Harrison, judging the temper of the crowd, said, "Compromise. Give you half an hour. Don't think we'll have the scaffold all fixed much short of that anyhow. Boy, boy, where's my Old Stonehouse Bourbon, the queen of Kentucky whiskies, aged ten long years in the wood?"

Malloy worked his way through the crowd and said, "What the devil? Get that man hanged."

"It's not the will of the sovereign majority," said Judge Harrison, who really wanted to harangue the crowd on the subject of Kentucky whisky.

"I said get it done. You can deliver your whisky speech under his body." He made a joke: "You can recommend that his body be pickled in it."

"Very well," said Judge Harrison. "Recess adjourned. Proceed with the hanging. And make the rope good and stout like Old Stonehouse Bourbon, aged in the wood."

Malloy took charge of the execution. He told one man to place the rope over that awning timber, others to clear the way for a wagon to be backed in, this man to fetch a plank which would rest between the wagon and the platform for a drop. All went smoothly; the knot was tied and left swinging in the torchlight.

Several in the crowd, old California men, now objected, saying the condemned man would not be given a good drop.

"I believe in hanging," one of the California men kept saying over and over, "but I believe in giving 'em a good long drop. Why, he's got a bare eighteen inches."

Helped by this controversy, John had edged over with back to the rain barrel. It was almost full. It was cool against his back. He got his hands over the edge and sank them deeply into the water. No one noticed. The rawhide was still tight, but its hard edge quickly softened. It became slick against his wrists. He kept working his arms and hands with a steady back-and-forth movement, feeling the rawhide loosen as it grew wet.

"Bring the prisoner," said Malloy.

"Half an hour!" shouted John. "I got twenty minutes yet."

"Your half hour started in the Montana House."

A man from the crowd shouted, "It started when you bushwhacked them poor boys over in Whisky Gulch!"

"Whisky Gulch be damned!" It was a new voice and new tone, and for the moment it drew everybody's attention. The speaker was a tall young man in a Union cavalry hat. He came through the crowd, pushing men this way and that, trying to get to the platform. He couldn't make the platform, so he climbed up the front wheel of the freight wagon and balanced there. "Yes, Whisky Gulch be damned. That's a frame-up."

"They found the gold on him!" a man brayed in a jackass voice.

"I'll tell you why he's being hanged—not because of any ambush or killing or robbery, but because there's a fellow here in town wants him out of the way."

"Malloy?" someone jeered.

"No, not Malloy. He's just a ten-penny errand boy for Lawford Hames. It's Hames, of course!" He thrust out an arm toward the western ridge and White Pine which lay beyond it. "Ask those farmers over there about Hames. Ask them about Big Hole Pass and the renegades that tried to cut their wagon outfit to pieces. A sweet deal. Oh, a sweet one! Saddle horses and guns for renegade Indians. Freight wagons and draft stock for Hames to go back into the freight business."

"Who the hell believes a pack of Pikes Peakers?"
Malloy called, really concerned now because some of
the crowd were actually listening to this fellow.
"Those sodbusters always have fought the miners."

Hackven added, "Yah, try to run us off our claims.
The claims we staked and sweated and slaved for. Already happened to me. Happen to you next. How'd
you like 'em to come along with their government
papers and say, 'Git, pull up stakes, this is punkin'-
raising ground'?"

They started taking sides, and naturally it was mostly the miners' side.

"Like in Californy," said one of them. "I had the
sweetest thing you ever see, and a pack of sodbusters
made me stop, claimed I was ruining their damn potato patches with tailings."

The young fellow tried to protest. He tried to say
that this had nothing to do with mining. He wanted to
talk about Hames. How come, he shouted, had Hames
all of a sudden got hold of half the freight business
coming in and out of all the Shauvegan diggings? He
knew all about Hames. Hames had been the man who
robbed his father.

"Who the hell are you?" asked the California man.

"I'm Pelton! Yes, I'm old Rawhide Pelton's boy. I
know all about Hames . . ." But nobody would listen
to him. They dragged him off the side of the wagon.
He was frightening the horses. He was making the
wagon move around so they couldn't lay the plank
right.

"What's wrong with you?" demanded the sweating,
tobacco-chewing, big-mustached man who owned the
freight wagon. "Don't you want this fellow to get a
good drop?"

John was thankful for the delay. It gave him a few
extra minutes to soak the rawhide. He twisted his
hands, deep sunk in the barrel. The rawhide had softened. It became slick like strips of boiled tripe. It had
stretched so he would have had no trouble slipping his
hands out. He did not do it, though. He moved and

lifted his hands from the water. He let water run from the tips of his fingers. He waited for something to divert everyone's attention.

It came unexpectedly when some exuberant miner fired a gun in the air. Everyone looked. Even Hackven, near by, with his gun drawn, turned to look.

And John twisted his hands free of the rawhide and lunged head foremost off the platform.

"Look out, thar he goes!" a man shouted.

Long on edge from the press and excitement, the team bolted. Men dived to escape. One man, caught momentarily underfoot, saved himself by clinging to the wagon tongue. The cursing driver, yelling, "Whoa! Whoa!" hung to the reins and was dragged with boot heels furrowing the ground.

John came up in the crowd. Excitement hid him. He might have escaped in that direction, only he wanted his guns back. They were inside the Judge's office, on his desk.

He crossed the platform, ducked through the door, grabbed up his Navies, and almost ran into Judge Harrison, who was coming from the rear of the building where he had been enjoying an ounce or two of Old Stonehouse Bourbon.

The Judge made a grab for him, and John hurled him out of his way. The Judge backpedaled, hit the wall, and sat down with his legs stiff out and his eyes staring. For seconds he was too stunned to speak or call for help, and by then John was through the rear door.

"Out back, out back!" called the Judge, but in the excitement, few heard him.

Outside, John was faced by a cut-away bank twenty feet high. He would need a ladder to climb that bank.

He ran down a narrow alley with the rear ends of buildings on one side and the bank on the other. He tried the rear door to a Chinese washee. Barred. He beat on it with his fist. Inside he could hear the excited talk of Chinese in their heathen tongue.

"Good fliend Chinee boy!" called John, but they would not let him in.

"Thar he is!" Hackven bellowed.

He was caught in a volley. He went to one knee, a Navy in each hand, and sent them diving for cover.

"Wa-hoo!" cried Comanche John, "Come along and bring your deppitys. It's suppertime and I'm serving red-hot biscuits. They lie a bit heavy on the stomach but I guarantee 'em to last a lifetime."

A bullet ripped through boards, a bullet cuffed wind against his cheek. He went sidewise, retreated, and came up again, this time behind a pile of fire-wood.

Someone was crawling toward him. Hackven. Hackven came up for a pot shot, and John put him down again with one ear and a large bit of hatbrim taken away.

"Don't press, boys, thar's enough for one and all," whooped John. He hopped up and did a war dance, kicking dust with his jackboots. "Ye know who I be? Waal, listen and I'll tell ye. I'm Comanche John from Yuba Gulch. I was born in Pike County, Missouri, and raised on catfish and corn likker. I pick my teeth with the cactus bush and drink water out of the crick like a horse. Last winter I craved raw meat and was plumb out o' bullets so I lit into a grizzly ba'r with my teeth. So if ye should see a three-legged grizzly, gave him room because he dee-tests the sight o' man."

He retreated. The narrow alley was his advantage now, for although he was badly outnumbered, *one* of them would have to be the first to show himself in the ten-foot space between the washee and the perpendicular bank.

The advantage was short-lived. Others were on the run to bottle him. Others atop the bank. He glimpsed one and hit him with bullet lead. The fellow lay cursing and kicking and calling for help and the sound of his bellowing tempered any foolhardiness that others might have shown.

At this end of the street, Shauvegan creek curved in against the bank. It left scant room for buildings, even little ones, and so they were built with their front ends on piles and their rears ending in cellars.

There was a slot between two of them, a catwalk. He did not dare place himself on the walk for fear of bullets from in front. He went beneath, climbed among strut poles, got to the ground, slid on the seat of his trousers with his boot heels to brake him, and ended almost in the muddy water of the creek.

There was a bridge; the road was yonder on the far side. He climbed, made the road. Pursuit had been all around him and now, suddenly, it was far away. He walked up a side street. He chose a horse from a hitch-rack and rode from town, not triumphant at his escape but sadly thinking how he had failed the Parson.

"But I'll come back," he said. "I'll come back and serve that Hames. I will, or I'm not the man they wrote the song about!"

CHAPTER SIXTEEN

COMANCHE JOHN rode to the Frenchman's ranch, where he found his gunpowder roan pony. From there he ranged far. He prospected; he rode guard with a freight outfit traveling to the Bow River in Canada. The gold country was somewhat stirred up about him after New Boston, and he saw two reward posters, but then things quieted. Word got around that he had been killed trying to rob a coach at Pistol Rock on the Snake.

He drew his pay from the freight boss and rode south again, to Redrock, Last Chance, Confederate, the Three Forks, and finally, by dark, to the White Pine.

The farmers were gone. The fur-company buildings now housed a shebang, and music could be heard all night. It wasn't the Parson's hymn music, either. He located O'Donnell, who had gone to mining. They'd pulled out early that summer, he said, after the placer outfits started dumping tailings across their fields, and had settled at Dutchman's Flat, where they had put in a few late crops.

"How's Hames?" he asked.

Hames was going bigger than ever; he had sold out the Shauvegan Gulch end of his freight and coach line at a huge profit and was now interesting himself in the new traffic to some silver mines at Ruby on the other side of Windigo Ridge.

"Any man's a fool who will quit a gold camp for a silver camp," O'Donnell said.

"No, it's placer first and then the hardrock," John said. "That was the history of Californy, it's coming to pass in Coloraydo, and next it'll come here. Hames is a couple of things I might lay my tongue to out o' the company of gentlemen, but he's no fool."

He asked about Pelton, the tall young lad who had spoken up for him the night of the trial. He would like to find Pelton. They had something in common. They both despised the very brass-lined intestines of Mr. Lawford Hames. Pelton had been seen just a week back in one place, and three or four days back at another, so John set out to trail him.

He had ridden all day, and now it was late afternoon. The sun was up, but not even its general position could be detected through a thick, cold layer of clouds. He kept his gunpowder roan pony at a slow jog down the little gulch; he rode with his head tilted slightly back, eyes almost closed but watching the country, his nose to the wind like an old woolly-wolf's. The air was sharp from snow higher up in the hills; it smelled of autumn pines and spruces, of frost-touched poplars and chokecherries. It smelled of the long cold to come.

It made him shake a chill from his shoulders and fasten the tie strings of his buckskin jacket.

Heavy clothes made him seem shorter and broader than before. His hair and whiskers retained no mark of their barbering the spring before; in places he had worked on himself with a bowie knife, but it was not what one would call a smooth job. He wore the same black slouch hat. His jacket was Sioux buckskin that he had traded for with a bull driver; he wore natural-mix homespun pants thrust into the tops of his old jackboots. The boots were pulled up to protect his knees from the thorns that grew in tangles, choking every gulch in Montana Territory. Around his waist on crossed belts, hitched high for riding, was the old brace of Navy sixes, Colt manufacture, .36 caliber. He carried a bowie, of course, and a powder and ball dispenser, and in a scabbard beneath his saddle, a Jaeger rifle.

> *"Oh, gather 'round, ye teamster men,*
> *And listen unto me,*
> *Whilst I sing of old Comanche John,*
> *The fastest gun thar be,"*

he sang in a monotone, just loud enough to be doing something.

> *"He robs the coach, he robs the bank,*
> *He robs the Union mail,*
> *And he's left his private graveyards*
> *All along the Bannock Trail."*

The small gulch led him to a large one, deep and steep, with timber and talus slopes and, after that, cliff summits. High yonder the pines looked purple and the rock like gray chalk. And there was a road—the stage road to Jackass City, and to Ruby, the new silver bonanza camp across still another ridge of mountains.

He drew rein at the edge of a creek. His chawing ceased, and suspicion showed in the sag of his shoulders. He had heard nothing, but a streak of muddy water hanging to the bank, slowly diluting in the clear water, told him that the bottom had been disturbed during the five or six minutes just past.

He listened. He nudged the pony, left the trail, rode quietly through brush, reaching far ahead to part, here and there, some branches. Then the pony made a twitch that warned him; he grunted, "Yep!" and dismounted.

Leaving the pony behind, he walked quietly, circling back to the road. He stopped. He had caught sight of a horse, saddled and bridled, tied in the deep bushes. And a second later a man appeared.

He was a tall man, his body covered by a blanket, a black kerchief tied to the brim of his hat. The kerchief was not quite down. John glimpsed his face—moved with surprise. It was young Buck Pelton, the man he had been looking for.

John did not reveal himself. He got comfortable and waited. He knew what the fellow was about—he intended to rob a Hames coach—but John wanted to see how he carried it off.

Pelton kept moving nervously, looking this way and that, feeling of his pistols. One of the spots he looked at was above, where he had placed an old hat and a shotgun among rocks so it might seem that he had a partner helping him. It was a fair job, John conceded, but the trick was worn out and not likely to fool any of the old coach hands making the run into Jackass City.

Comanche John was critical, and a little sad. Obviously this fellow was poor shakes as a road agent, and the days of the poor-shake road agent were short and full of bullet lead. It was too bad. It was, for young Pelton had a good, clean-cut look about him, he had a proud way with his shoulders, and he had the manner of a man who liked his horse.

Then, from high on the side of the gulch, came a clatter of hoofs and wheels—the coach was coming.

The young man looked frightened. He pulled his mask down, drew both Navies, and got out of sight.

It was quiet now, so quiet that the sounds of the creek came through, the gurgle and echo of water over stones. The coach was passing through deep timber and it could be heard only when the road swung out around the rock faces of the mountain.

Then suddenly it was there. It rattled and banged. It was in view, topheavy, careening to the creek, fording it, out of sight briefly, then climbing again, water streaming from its wheels, the driver in the high seat, the shotgun guard beside him with a rifle clamped between his knees.

"Why, damn *him,*" John said, seeing the guard. It was Sanchez.

A bend in the road hid the obstruction until the last second. The lead team saw it and made a lunge into the chokecherry bramble. With a curse, the driver was on his feet, going for the brake.

"Hands up!" shouted young Pelton, appearing in the road, his Navies angled upward at the driver and Sanchez.

The coach stopped suddenly. Sanchez, halfway to his feet, reeled and grabbed for balance. He had his sawed-off shotgun half lifted, hidden by his body and the driver, and the abrupt jerk of the coach probably saved the young man's life.

The teams, tangling and at cross purposes, climbed one another's rumps, and the driver, with a mighty, cursing dexterity, managed to control them. To make things worse, some of the passengers were trying to get outside, some were trying to hide, and all of them were shouting at once.

"Keep quiet in there, damn you, there's no extra charge for this!" the driver bellowed.

"What's going on?" a thin, angry, gray-haired gentleman asked, head out of the window. "Driver, what's the meaning of this?"

"You git your head back in or it's likely to be chopped off by a bullet. It's a holdup, same as usual. I been—"

"Hands up!" cried young Pelton.

"Why, you damn idiot! You want me to git my

hands up and turn my horses loose? Have me lose coach, baggage, and all? Then where'd you be? You do your job and let me tend to mine."

He had gee-hawed the teams into a zigzag sort of stability and sat down, foot on the brake. "Don't pint them guns at me, ye fool," he said. "You shoot *me* and then who's going to control these Injun mules?"

"Get down!" Pelton said to Sanchez. Sanchez started to obey, using the far side, but the masked man was too alert for that. "*This* side." He pointed to the hat and gun muzzles above. "Don't try anything. I'm not alone."

"*Si*, I try nothing." And Sanchez very ostentatiously keeping his arms wide, slid down the near side.

"Hold the lead team."

"*Si*." Sanchez still carried a gun. He had an Army model Colt tied down on his right leg. The weight of it made him seem to limp a trifle as he went forward, but he kept turned to hide the gun, and he succeeded.

The whiskered man, chawing nervously, whispered, "Git the gun, ye young idjit, git the gun!"

But Pelton did not see the gun. He moved far over against the slant of the mountain, where he tried to watch everybody at once.

"Climb out, all of you!" he called to the passengers.

A heavy, flushed man was the first to emerge. A couple of miners followed; a seedy, dressed-up man; then the elderly man, spare, gray, brittle-looking; and a girl, very pretty, about nineteen years old; and there were two other men and a woman.

The girl's skirt had caught on the iron step. She tore it. The young road agent started forward, apparently with a gentleman's instinct that asserted itself even here.

"Stay away from me!" she cried.

The elderly gentleman freed her dress, took her arm, said some words of reassurance. They were very similar in profile, and it was easy to guess that she was his daughter or granddaughter.

"Line up!" the robber said, swinging his Navies.

"Don't point your guns at me!" the girl cried. "Don't—"

"Nettie!" the gentleman said.

Sanchez held the lead team. His left side was in view. Very slowly he lowered his right hand. He did it with a creepy, smooth movement, straight down, so that it was hidden from the young man's view. Now, using only hand, wrist, and forearm, he lifted the revolver from its holster. He held it with the barrel toward the ground. He had yet to turn and point it. He started this very casually, looking not at his quarry, but at the horses. A half-second more and Pelton would have been a dead man.

"No, ye don't!" muttered Comanche John, his words ending in explosion as he drew and fired.

Sanchez was hit and knocked from his feet. He lay bullet-shocked with the team threatening to trample him.

"Stay whar ye be!"

The voice of the black-whiskered man stopped everyone. The young robber spun around.

"Stay on your job! Git back to it, lad. Now maybe they'll believe when ye tell 'em you're not alone."

Sanchez lay on his right side, a bleeding right arm on the ground. He got hold of the arm and pressed to stop the blood. He got groggily to his knees. He looked around baffled.

"Hello, Sanchez," said John, his voice just reaching him, but with a quality that cut through the shock that glazed his mind. "My advice is git back to barbering."

Sanchez made words with his lips, but no sound. He kept looking for the voice.

"Don't bother," John said in a low growl. "I can see you and that's all we need. Shouldn't be a surprise I'm hyar. *Said* I'd come gunning your hide if ye told my name wasn't Smith. Had to let you off easy with only an arm. That's because I shot from the unseen. Give ye a second chance. Name is *Smith*. Comanche John be dead and buried, and I'd advise ye never again to forget it."

Sanchez said not a word. He cared for his shattered arm, getting it inside his shirt, and his belt cinched around it. Pain made him clench his large yellow teeth. John watched him—and everybody. He remained in the brush, a Navy ready, though he didn't expect he'd need to use it.

"Git on with the robbery, lad," he said.

Young fellow too nervous, no idea how to conduct a robbery, no idea at all. Now and then John dropped a word of advice, but quietly, not wanting to embarrass him.

"Keep the coach door open. Make 'em line up straight, military."

The driver, craning, trying to get a glimpse of John, said, "Say, you robbed me down in I-de-ho."

"Never mind about me, you watch the horses. Lad, forget about robbing the passengers. Idee in coach robbery is to get the *good will* of the passengers. Give your average passenger a halfway chance, he'll end up his journey feeling better toward the road agent than he does toward the company. That's because the road agent treated him fair and the company didn't. Fetch the strongbox. No, not you, give the job to somebody. Pick a passenger. Fat passenger is best. That'n yonder in the gaiters. Your fat passenger naturally moves slower, and he won't want to miss his supper. I do hope that strongbox ain't riveted to the floor because if so we'll have to burn the coach to git it."

The box was not riveted down. The fat man, grunting and wheezing, pulled it out and dumped it. It struck with a heavy, metallic clank. There was no use demanding the key because it would be at the express office in Jackass City.

"That's all, job finished," said John. "Send 'em on their way." And in another minute the coach, with all back aboard, was rolling away, pulling the steep mountain grade.

Comanche John thereupon slouched into view. He

spat and looked sad and said, "Son, you'll never come much closer than that to being kilt."

The young man did not answer. He pulled off his kerchief, revealing a face beaded and streaked with sweat. He was too trembly to stand. He sat down on a rock and breathed, steadying himself.

John said, "Put the Navies back before they explode and blow your toes off."

Young Pelton did, poking several times to find the holsters. He now noticed something familiar about John. He sat staring up at him.

"I've seen you before."

"Why, so ye have. New Boston. A party. I war scheduled to give an ex-e-bition o' treading on air with the help of a cravat, only fate gave me the chance to dee-cline the offer."

"You're Comanche John!"

"The same. Oh, I don't wonder ye don't recognize me. Had just had a haircut and beard trim then, banker-style. Springtime. Let her grow since. Winter pelage. Winter hyar in this country a man needs all the hair he can grow."

"First coach I ever robbed!" whispered Pelton, preoccupied.

"Lad, ye needn't have told me. Would have been your last, too. What you trying to do, git even with Hames? I tell ye, this robbery will prove to be a mighty slow way."

They pried the strongbox open. It contained neither money nor bullion, nothing of value except a few trinkets addressed to a jeweler in Ruby, over the Windigo Pass.

Comanche John sat down on the box in disgust and said, "Son, what possessed ye to choose this particular coach?"

"I just took my chance."

"Chance! No planning, headwork, nothing. That's how the young generation goes about things. No money in those baubles. Just evidence, enough to git ye hung."

They rode away together, the young man tall and straight in the saddle, the older one giving and sagging with each move of his horse, following the brush of the bottoms, and then a deer trail up the mountain.

The coach was long since out of sight. The sun shone pale for a while, then it faded among clouds near the horizon. As they climbed, a cold wind found them. It was a frigid reminder of the lateness of the season, making Comanche John hide his hands inside his jacket to keep them warm.

When they stopped to breathe their horses, he said, "That true ye be Rawhide Pelton's boy?"

The young man nodded. "Say, are you a friend of Dad's?"

"That's not quite the word for it." Comanche John looked at him balefully and took his hands from his jacket to feel along the smooth-worn Navy butts. "Fact is, you being his boy don't recommend you to me a-tall. That damn Rawhide Pelton was the first man to put sleeper guards inside his stagecoaches disguised as honest passengers."

"All's fair in—"

"And I say *no*. All ain't fair. There's a right and a wrong way to everything, a brave way and a sneakin' way, and I say a sleeper guard is a low, ornery trick on a road agent. O' course I speak unbiased; I given up coach robbery, took religion, hit the sawdust trail, figuring on finding me a Blackfoot gal and spending my last years in peace. Got nothing at stake. Just like to see things run on the square. And when I think of poor old Tom Tate lying dead in his grave on Sky-U road, riddled with buckshot by a sleeper guard on your pappy's coach! Made up a verse about him. Teamsters did. Verse in my song. You heared my song, haven't ye?"

Young Pelton shook his head.

"Ignorance! Young man, I can see you won't git along too well in this country until ye pay a mind to principle, give thought to the important people, trailblazers, men that chased out the Injuns. Now, I'll sing a bit to ye."

They rode on, following a trail through sparse timber, around a big bulge of the mountain, with the black-whiskered man singing:

> "*Thar was Comanche John and Silcox*
> *And Buckshot Tommy Tate,*
> *And before the autumn it was o'er*
> *They all had met their fate;*
> *They shot Silcox in Denver,*
> *And poor Tommy got the same,*
> *Whilst Comanche took religion*
> *And tried to change his name.*"

John stopped, blasted tobacco juice into the wind, and explained: "Smith's the name I been going under. Then betimes I use another name, *Jones*. They're both good, but I think I prefer Smith to Jones. It's not so unusual. That's another thing ye got to pay heed to if ye take up robbery as a profession."

The trail was wider here, and they rode stirrup to stirrup.

John went on talking, his head down, the wind bending his black slouch hat over his face. "A man does have to be careful about the names he picks. Say ye choose to call yourself by an unusual name like Beauregard. Well, right off if there happens to be another Beauregard within three sleeps and two mountain ranges he can't rest until he's off to see ye and find out if you're of the New Orleans Beauregards or the Natchez Beauregards, and, o' course, he learns that you're neither. But the Smiths don't care, and it's been my notice that the Joneses don't give a damn, neither."

They rode over the ridge into a wind that precluded conversation, that caught words and whipped them away so a man had to shout to be heard. Later the wind carried pellets of snow that stung when they hit. The trail dropped into the timber and there they found shelter again.

"I'm not a snooper," Comanche John said, "but I must say I'm a bit curious what Hames did to your pa."

"They were half and half in Kansas and Colorado. Dad was sick, came to St. Louis to be doctored. I was in the army. When they discharged me with a rifle ball in my hip I heard that the company was bankrupt. I suspected Hames then, but Dad didn't. He blamed himself, his sickness, said it was because he wasn't on the job to help. He said that Hames was honest, he'd stake his life on it. I almost believed him. I went to Denver City when I was able to, thought I could save something. We'd been sold out. In the meantime Hames went to California and had the money to start up business on his own. Now he's here, bigger than ever."

"He went broke somewhere along the way. When I first run onto him yonder in I-de-ho, he didn't know if a bank-note was colored red, white, or brindle. He didn't even own the horse he was riding. He'd stole it somewhere."

"Well, he robbed my dad!"

"Shore up your temper, lad, I'm not doubting that." John kept talking, mostly about Hames, and what a skunk he was, a regular damn civet cat. "When I think of him, robbing his best friend and partner, and that partner old and sick in St. Loo, and that partner's own son in the army, fighting for the Confed'racy—"

"The Union."

Comanche John turned away from him. He had suddenly gone sour on all the world. He slapped his old, black hat flatter on his head and blasted tobacco juice at a porphyry boulder and cursed.

"Why is it," he asked, addressing the mountainside, "when I come riding along, and see some ignorant Yankee trying to rob a coach, ready to be kilt, when I see something like that, why don't I just go along and mind my own business? Now here's a fellow, son of the man that deadfalled my best friend, a fellow so ignorant he's not even heared the most popular song in the whole Nor'west, and I save *him*, rescue him, when by all the laws of judgment and good decency I ought to kill him myself. By grab, I *do* need a squaw to take care o' me, because it looks like my brains have jellied."

Pelton allowed his horse to lag so he could have a laugh without John noticing, and John said, "Oh, don't sulk. After all, it's not your fault you're a damn-Yank. It's the way you was brung up."

They rode side by side as an early darkness settled. Miles off, across a creek valley, were the lights of a town.

"Jackass City," said John. "Gold diggings. Rich, but pockety. That ridge, that's the Windigo. Ruby on t'other side. Not far, eight-ten mile. Plenty will be heard o' Ruby. She'll be the biggest silver camp north of the Comstock when the veins are opened. Ruby silver, I've seen it, lumps big as so, red as blood and heavy as bullet metal. That's what Hames is aiming for, Ruby and not that poor-scratch camp o' Jackass City. I 'low there'll be three thousand men in Ruby come next spring. And that gives me an idee."

He did not divulge his idea, but he kept thinking about it and added, "Great opportunity. Make a million. And beat Hames at the same time."

"Well?" said Buck, growing impatient.

"Heavy freight to those mines—quicksilver, salt, amalgamators, stamp mills, cable, stuff like that. Great opportunity for a freighting man. That's *you*, you're a freight man. Understand book work. With my help. No, I'm no freight man, but I know the country. I been over it backward and forward, know every hump and hollow." John pointed to the high, snowy ridge beyond Jackass as he talked. "Now, I been yonder and back again, and I learned a thing or three. I learned about the Windigo Pass."

"If it's a good road, then Hames has already claimed it."

"That's just the point, it's no road at all."

Hames, John explained, was using the Elk Creek

road. Now the Elk Creek road was fine, except that it took the long, winding way around, and always snowed deep in winter—but the Windigo!

"You mean we could grab the Windigo route and freight over it?"

"Could."

Pelton suddenly reined in. "What mining company is it in Ruby—the London and Montana?"

"Why, yes, I do believe—"

"Of course! The London and Montana! That's why he sold the New Boston line and came here!"

He explained how it was to Comanche John. The Pelton and Hames company had an agreement with the L. & M. They were headed into new territory and needed a freight agreement. Pelton and Hames guaranteed the wagons and they guaranteed the tonnage. Pelton, Sr., put the deal through. Now Hames was here to put the old contract in force.

John said, "If Pelton and Hames put the deal through, why—"

"Of course, it's as much my contract as Hames's! And you're in it with me, half and half."

John gloated about it as he rode. "Me in the freight business! By dang. I can just *see* me. Office, spring-seat chair. Desk and a spittoon. Black serge suit and congress gaiters. Watch and chain. Lad, we'll beat that cheating, robbing Lawford Hames at his own game."

"We'll break him, and then I'll break his neck."

John whooped. "We'll whipsaw him and flimflam him and we'll weight him with lead from a Navy Colt. Go tell the Blackfoot maidens to wait because I got one last fling in my hide and I'm going to cut myself a slice of fortune whilst making it."

CHAPTER SEVENTEEN

THEY FOLLOWED THE STAGE ROAD. At lower altitudes the snow disappeared and became a trickle of water in the ruts. In the valley bottom it was mud. They followed a creek, thick yellow from placer workings higher up. Prospectors' shanties and dugouts had been built along the sides of the gulch. The road climbed through pines, dropped over a shoulder of ground, and there were the lights of Jackass City.

It was a larger camp than John had expected, for it had boasted only a dozen cabins on his last visit. Placer mining had spread from the gulch bottom to the benches and had pushed the town up the slope, here and there undermining the main street itself so trestles or log cribworks were necessary to keep it from caving in. It was cold; the hoof-punched muck of the street had commenced to freeze, not deeply, only at the surface, enough to make a brittle sound under the hoofs of the horses. Only a few people about, hurrying from one place to another. Apparently no excitement because of the robbery.

They passed a large, two-story hotel, the Overland. Uphill, at the end of a narrow street, was a feed stable.

"Town seems safe enough," said John. "Anyhow, they wouldn't expect holdup men *here*, under their very noses."

At the feed stable, a young Negro, smartly attired in a steamboat officer's uniform, let the gate down.

"Hear the news?" he asked cheerfully. "Old stagecoach she's robbed again."

"Ag'in?" cried John. "What's the country coming to? Who's the sheriff here? Ain't ye got a vigilance committee, a miners' meeting? Whyn't the law clean those varmints out? I dunno whether I feel safe in this town or not. You keep my horse saddled, understand? Take the saddle off and curry him and feed him and put it back on again. I got an idee I'll just be passing through."

He limped from the stiffness of long riding in the cold, and was still limping when they were downhill to the plank sidewalk in front of the Overland. A high, ornate awning had been attached to the front of the building, and there were green-painted benches for guests to sit on, but nobody was there tonight. The front windows were misted over. John lagged behind his companion, letting him reach the door first and go inside first.

"I got no fancy for this place," John said.

"Big freight operators. Only the best!"

The lobby was low and wide, with a huge pillar in the middle. Most of the light came from bracket lamps on the four sides of the pillar. Men were seated on the lounge side of the room, dripping mud off their boots and spitting tobacco juice wherever they pleased, doing it in a prosperous way which showed they were mine owners, boss freighters, or at the very least, paying guests.

John did not recognize a soul.

"Four walls, thick ones, too. Last time I saw walls this thick it war a jail."

A small, quick-eyed man, dressed all in black except for his shirt, had appeared behind the desk.

"I assume, sir," said Buck Pelton, looking him cold in the eye, "that dinner is still available."

The man straightened, recognizing quality when it appeared before him, and said, "Oh, yes, on special order, *sir!* Would you like to register for rooms, *sir?*"

Comanche John looked all around, his black slouch hat far over his eyes. "What's your charges?" he asked.

"Ten dollars a night," the clerk said. "Unless you want the cheaper rooms, then—"

"Cheaper! Hell's fire, who ye think you're talking to?" He shot tobacco juice at a brass spittoon and missed it. "Poor grade o' spittoon. I dunno. That price —it's pretty low to what we been used to. Me and my partner, we're big freight operators, backed by British capital, nat'ally used to the best. Feather ticks, pillows, quilts, all that. Maybe we should sample the grub hereabouts first."

The clerk said, "As you wish," and pointed the way to the dining room.

"You carried that off in fine style," said young Pelton.

"Oh, I been around a mile or three in my time. Been to San Francisco, Denver City, Hannibal. Not much of a man for hotels, though. Beds bend a man in the middle, weaken his spine. Don't do a gun bar'l a bit o' good to bend 'er in the middle, and neither does it a man's spine. You know what the best bed in the world is? Spruce boughs with a buffalo robe on good mountain soil. You lie on a bed like that, real straight, with your toes pointed down, and ye can feel the tiredness pick up and flow out of ye whilst your body sucks new strength out of the soil."

John talked to fill the time while walking to the dining room. They passed through a cloak closet where Buck hung up his sheared-beaver hat; but John did not leave *his* hat, that old black slouch was part of his disguise.

The main dining room had a single large table down the middle. Places were all set, the plates upside down, with napkins, knives, and forks ready for breakfast. There was an arch and a second dining room beyond—the "quality" dining room with private tables, and up some steps to a slightly higher level, a row of booths with silk screens that could be folded out for privacy.

A Chinese boy came running to say, "Private table, sure, much obliged, come quick please."

"We be getting mighty deep in this cave," John muttered.

One of the booths was occupied. Comanche John, shorter, and lagging behind, felt Buck's hesitation of surprise and guessed who it would be. It was the girl and the old gentleman of the stagecoach, and there was a third person—Lawford Hames.

I have walked into it now, thought Comanche John. It naturally occurred to him that it might be best to shoot it out with Hames and be done with him. But there was that girl yonder, and the old gentleman, and there was something in Hames's eyes—something which indicated that this meeting was as unwelcome to him as it was to John.

"Buck!" cried Hames, getting to his feet, sounding delighted.

"Hello, Lawford," Buck said, smiling but savage about it—not really trying to hide what he felt. Buck said to Comanche John, "This is Mr. Lawford Hames; have you ever met him?"

"Can't re-collect having had the de-stinction," said John. "Smith is the handle."

"Glad to know you, Smith," said Hames, and John knew that for the moment he was safe. Hames had the same understandable desire to hide his past that John did.

"Well, Buck!" Hames went on. He smiled, showing his strong teeth. He came down to shake hands. "I'd heard you were in the country. Why haven't you come around before?" He turned to the girl and the old man. "Nettie, this is Buck Pelton. Miss Nettie Bowden. And P. R. Bowden—Mr. Pelton. This is Mr. Pelton's son, you know, my former partner."

Buck spoke to the girl and the man. Only a few hours before he had seen them over the muzzle of his pistol, but neither appeared to suspect his identity.

"Miss Bowden and her father have had an unnerving experience," Hames said. "The coach carrying them here was robbed on the other side of the pass."

"The scoundrels!" Bowden said, nervous and fierce. "Shot down the guard in cold blood. Only an accident he wasn't killed. I tell you, there'll have to be a law in this country, an effective law, if we're going to attract much foreign capital."

"Did you lose anything?" Buck asked.

"They didn't rob the passengers," said Miss Nettie. She had a low, sweet voice, and John could tell by her eyes that she was interested in Buck. Well, what gal wouldn't be?

Hames noticed it, too, and it was obvious that he didn't like it.

"Won't you and Mr. Smith join us?" Hames asked. "We can move two of these tables together."

"I just happened to notice," John said, backing off, "that I came hyar to supper without my white linen shirt on."

He had seen somebody in the coatroom, and it was like seeing a ghost. Maybe he *had* seen a ghost, the ghost of Moose Petley, Moose of the ox-yoke mustache, who was supposed to be dead over on the Big Hole.

"Then you join us, Buck!" said Hames.

"I'd better not."

"Well, later. Tomorrow. Buck, we'll have to talk over old times. What are you doing, Buck? How are you engaging yourself. Mining?"

"The only thing I know—freight."

"Oh!" said Hames, lifting his eyebrows. "Well, competition is what keeps us all out of the mud, isn't it? Frankly, though," and he showed tolerance and contempt, "I never heard of your freight line. Where is it?"

"One of these days," said John in his easy drawl, getting in before young Pelton grew angry at the other man's tone and started a brawl, "one of these days you'll open up your eyes and won't even be able to believe what ye see."

"You have something planned for me, don't you?" Hames's voice was very soft and very deadly. "You're keeping it for a surprise. Well, good. Have to it! It may be I'll have a surprise for you, too."

"If ye don't mind," said John, getting Buck under the arm and pulling him along, "I *would* like to go back for that white linen shirt."

Whatever Buck had had in mind to say, the feel of John's grasp dissuaded him.

"I wish you would dine with us," said the old gentleman, who evidently had not noticed how taut the situation had become.

But Buck begged they be excused, and John, turning, had a wary look at the coatroom. Moose Petley was no longer in sight.

"What's the trouble?" Buck asked, annoyed at being dragged away. "I'm not going to run from—"

"O' course not. But there's always a time and place, and this ain't it. This is *his* place. I'd ruther tackle a grizzly out on the trail than a skunk in his own burrow. Here he had us for'ard and back. Unless the thing I just saw was a ghost."

"What do you mean?"

"Man, supposed to be dead with his bones picked by wolves back along Big Hole Pass. Petley. Another of the old gang. That makes two, Petley and Sanchez, and I'll wager Hames has more of 'em in the bushes to call on if he needs. Yes, I'll wager Hames *will* have a surprise for us."

The appearance and prompt disappearance of Moose Petley had somewhat unnerved him. *He* had never actually seen Moose lying dead, but others had, men he believed. Could be a ghost, of course. There *were* ghosts. No use arguing about it like some people did. Back in Missouri they had ghosts. It had been proved a hundred times, but there they had old, established graveyards, and decayed houses to haunt, things a ghost really needed if he was going to amount to anything, but hereabouts a man never heard of ghosts, country was too new. Damn Pikes Peakers, bragged they'd seen him dead, wagon talk, teamster talk. Loudmouth teamster talk.

He was ready for Moose Petley as he passed through the cloak closet, and again when he entered the lobby. The men were there, the same loungers as before, yawning, talking, digging wax from their ears with matchsticks—those Blue Devil patent matches that lately were becoming commonplace in the gold camps—but not Moose.

"Why is it," John drawled as if Petley were the farthest thing from his mind, "when a man gits prosperous, the first thing he does is loaf in a hotel lobby and dig the wax from his ears?"

They stepped warily through the door to the platform sidewalk.

A rangy wolf dog had come sniffing along at the corners and now he stopped with ears cocked to look in the shadow between two small, log-shanty saloons, and John, watching the dog, said, "Yep! You stay back a bit."

"No, I'll—"

"Stay back. I need room. You're the lad that knows the wagon busines. I'm the half of the partnership that knows *this* sort of business."

He ambled along a few steps in front of Buck, down from the Overland's platform walk, along a stretch of pole corduroy, almost to where the dog stood with his hackles up.

John stopped close against the building. He spoke:

"Moose, come out o' thar or I'll drill ye right betwixt the eyes."

He could hear a startled movement. Then slowly the huge fellow plodded out of the darkness, along the narrow space hardly wide enough for his shoulders.

"Why, it's my old friend, John!" cried Moose, his ox-yoke mustache twitching with simulated pleasure. "I didn't know who you were."

"The hell you didn't."

" 'Pon my soul, no, I didn't."

"Why were ye waiting to bushwhack me? Just a habit ye formed?"

"I *wasn't*. I had plenty of chance to bushwhack you already if I'd been that kind. Oh, I kilt a couple of men in my day, might as well own up to it, but honest, fair and square, bullets in front, toe-to-toe. I mayn't ever had religion, but I got my code."

John kept watch of him. He looked Moose up and

down, all the six-feet-two, two hundred pounds of him.

"What were you doing inside that hotel?"

"I live there!"

"Oh, live thar be damned! Look at ye—haven't had a bath since ye fell overboard in the Sacramento back in '54. Lice on ye. You couldn't live in a hotel."

"That's a lie. I bathed just last year at a barbershop down in Boise City."

"I known first-class livery barns that wouldn't tolerate a man like you sleeping in their stalls, leave alone a hotel like the Overland. I know why you was thar. Ye be working for Hames."

Moose Petley opened his mouth to say no, but he decided not to.

"I should shoot ye," John muttered, angry at his own softness. "I should, and put it down as my good deed for the day."

"You wouldn't do that, John. We been through too much together. Sometimes we been on opposite sides, true, but we been through it. Old friends is the best friends, I always say. I learned my lesson at Big Hole. I'm a changed man. I'll admit my mistake, I'll admit I fell in with bad companions—Little Tom, Belly River Bob, and that lot, but I learned my lesson. I'm still carrying rifle lead from the Big Hole to remind me of that lesson. I tell ye, Comanche—"

"Name ain't Comanche. Name is Smith, or Jones, I don't care much which. You go shouting Comanche around hyar and git me hung, why I'll see to it you're hung, too. I could do it."

"I know you could do it," Moose said, pleading, "but men with marks agin' their names have to stick together. I'll keep quiet about it if you'll keep quiet."

Moose wanted to buy them a drink, but the offer was refused.

They got their horses and rode from camp. At an abandoned dugout shanty, they slept for a while. They got up and cooked breakfast. Back of them they could see Jackass City, misty and gray, with the smokes of early fires hanging to the treetops, spreading down the gulch. In the other direction rose the cold peaks of the Windigo Ridge.

"Our pass!" said Buck, and there was doubt in his voice. It looked steep and forbidding.

"Yep, our pass!"

They rode up the gulch, along a wagon road, to a cluster of cabins called Stumptown where some poor quartz veins were being developed. The road played out in half a dozen directions on the other side of Stumptown, and the two men found themselves in a grassy, cirquelike area with the mountain rising steeply on three sides.

"Main camp could be here," John said.

They rode on, along a trail. This, John pointed out, could be widened to make a road. He talked about Ruby City, over the pass, about the huge silver mines that British capital was developing, and about silver mines in general.

"I war at Comstock. Learned all about silver mines. Mills, pan amalgamators, stamps, hot steam jets, all that truck. Tell ye why they have to have our road, the year-around road—because something breaks down once a day and a steady stream of repair parts has to come or the mine goes bust. Knew a holdup man one time, used to waylay repair parts, hold 'em for ransom. Only one day he got a box marked 'Rush—Enjine Bearings' and it war fifty pounds of giant powder on a time fuse."

Steep as it was, John pointed out at their first rest, the Windigo was *the* winter road, because much of it would blow clear, and the bad places, where snow would settle in forty or fifty feet deep, were short and could be tunneled by snowsheds. Of course, there were the cliffs. Over the cliffs they'd need trestle.

"Build all that *this fall?*"

"I got friends. I got friends with more muscle and less brains than anybody you'd likely come onto this side of Ioway. Oh, even the dumbest of them, that Stocker, even *he* could dig road, build shed, shovel snow, see the advantage of a piece of road to charge toll on. That's the ticket—make every man of 'em an independent operator, only, o' course, we'll contract 'em, pay a certain amount per ton for each piece of road, and all at one place. It can be worked out. And these fellows, damn ragged Pikes Peakers, they got cause to dee-spise Hames, too. He run 'em off the White Pine, land they bought and paid for."

The mountain became steeper. They switchbacked toward a high peak from which the early snow had not melted. Great blocks of porphyry here covered the slope.

"I hope your Pikes Peakers have strong backs," said Buck.

"Nothing to it. Snakehole the big boulders, jump-shoot the smaller ones, giant powder, roll 'em down the hill."

"Where do we get giant powder?"

"On credit from Ruby."

Here it was alternating timber and stone. Glaciers of another age had scooped out a three-sided amphitheater with cliffs for walls. Far below lay a tiny lake.

"No place for a road here," Buck said.

"Why, no. You re-collect I said something about a trestle? Two hundred paces of trestle here saves ye six miles. And that, son, is one o' the ways we'll beat Hames. Oh, I can just see that Hames wallowing tail-deep to his mules up that Elk Creek road and hyar we'll be, the Pelton-Comanche Freight Lines pulling safe and solid across trestle and through snowshed tunnel, putting two hundred tons a day into Ruby regular like clockwork."

CHAPTER EIGHTEEN

THEY CROSSED THE PASS and rode down to the new camp of Ruby.

Ruby did not have a placer-camp look about it, it

had a hardrock look. In other words, you could tell there was capital at work.

The London & Montana had set up a sawmill, so everything was built of plank rather than log. The streets had been laid out by transit so things were going up in squares instead of just mushrooming anywhere. The whisky, however, was as bad as usual.

John told them plenty about the poor quality of their whisky compared with what he'd been used to while waiting for Buck to come back from his meeting with P. W. Hutton, resident manager of the London & Montana.

John waited a long time, and he expected the worst. "He tried to welsh on your half of that agreement?" he asked as soon as he had Buck by himself.

No, Hutton had not welshed. He had been surprised that the Pelton half of the old firm was still in business, but seeing it was, Hutton would see he got his share of freight. There would be enough for all. The mines at Ruby looked extremely good. The chief thing worrying Hutton had been the prospect of being isolated for weeks or months in the winter when snow sometimes reached depths of ten or twelve feet. And here was a young man, a levelheaded young fellow brought up in the freight business, wanting to guarantee him the delivery of a certain specific tonnage winter and summer, regardless of everything. He would, in fact, be willing to pay a premium, say $20 per ton, on "time freight" during the winter, provided Pelton would guarantee a minimum delivery of a hundred tons a week.

Caution made Buck draw back from this, fearing snowslide or some other unforeseen occurrence, so they compromised on two hundred tons each two-week period, Hutton guaranteeing this amount of freight, and Buck guaranteeing to deliver it.

In addition, with only a momentary hesitation, Hutton wrote him an order against the express bank for $8,000—payment in full for the November minimum.

But now that the deal was closed, John was curiously alarmed. "We'll have to build that road and *keep* it built, keep it open, too. By grab, I hope I made no mistakes. Say, whar we gitting wagons and stock?"

"That's my job. You build the road—you and your Pikes Peakers."

For wagons and stock, Buck sought a third partner in the enterprise, big, hunch-shouldered Frying Pan Murphy, once of Denver, his father's competitor, now crowded out of the lucrative Benton—Last Chance traffic when the Circle J outfit established a monopoly on the Wolf Creek toll road. Murphy, with his idle stock, would be willing to try anything.

John, in the meantime, rode to Dutchman's Flat, where, in a poor clutch of cabins surrounded by bitty gardens and spud patches, the remnants of the Parson's emigrant group were trying to make a living by supplying the near-by gold camps with fresh produce, but even with spuds at 25 cents a pound and snap beans at a dollar he could see they were having a mighty tough go of it.

A couple of kids and nine assorted dogs took note of his approach. The dogs were ferocious as starving wolves, and then of a sudden willing to wag their backsides out of joint when he dismounted and spoke a kind word. Each of the children he gave a bitty nugget. Women came to the doors of some of the shacks to shade their eyes and watch him, and one of them was the rangy and rawboned Widow Cobb.

"Lord be praised," cried the Widow Cobb, lifting both arms in a sign of blessed relief. "It's him, it's him, it's Smith and he ain't been hung after all."

"I warn't born to git hung. I already told ye—"

"Oh, but you're gaunt. Look at ye. You got no flesh on your bones. You been traveling with the wolf pack again. You strayed off the track of righteousness. We better send for the Parson because you need some gospel talked at you."

"I been washed by the blood and rectified by the spirit. I'm a pilgrim and weary, Sister Cobb."

"Set down." She got him inside and pulled him to a

stool. "Feel them arms. Oh, you're gaunt. I've seen jerky with more flab than you got!" She called one of the kids who was peeping inside. "Waldo, help this poor gentleman off with his boots. Now you set, and I'll cook a snack for you."

John sat, moaning from luxury, his feet h'isted, toes wiggling. "By grab, Sister Cobb, you'll spile me for heaven with this sort of treatment."

Stuffing wood in the fireplace, fanning it with her apron, she said, "I only hope you make that promised land, Brother John."

"I just go down the trail o' life, helping men with their loads, and it's true I have lifted the gold off some of 'em, but on t'other hand, gold is the heaviest thing thar is in the world, heavier than lead even, and the ruination of more men than whisky and chawing to-bacco put together. Remember how the Parson used to sing:

> "'Ye should help the weary pilgrim,
> Ye should lift his heavy load?'"

"He didn't mean gold, John. He meant the *spiritual* load, not lifting things with the help of a Navy six."

"Seek not the treasures of this world for they do cor-rupt and destroy. I tooken from the rich and given to the poor." And to prove the point, twitching his bare toes to keep time, he sang:

> "Now I sing of old Comanche John
> And his partner, Whisky Ike;
> The only motto that they had
> Was share and share alike;
> They robbed the bank at Uniontown
> And coaches three or four,
> They robbed the rich-unrighteous
> And they gave it to the pore."

The Widow Cobb had scant liking for the song. "What you need is a woman's care," she said. "You need to be mothered and patched and fatted up."

"Woman, I don't aim to wed until I made my mark in the world." She gave him such a stare he got his feet down and explained. "I'm in the freight business now. Yes, I am. Freight contract, wagons, stock, everything. All except a road. And that's whar you're going to help me. You and your Pikes Peakers. You're going to build road, trestle, and snowshed, and every man that builds will own his own stretch of road, and collect toll off'n it, and make himself a bit of money."

"You mean abandon our farms, the farms we worked for and slaved for—"

"It won't hurt to abandon 'em for the winter. Unless you're too lazy. Unless ye'd all rather sit the winter out in an easy chair."

"John, you know better'n that." She hung the kettle of congealed venison stew over the new fire and stood up to say, "If your offer is on the fair, then I accept it for 'em. I do, and I'll see to it ye get your workmen. You're right about sitting in a chair all winter, humping over a fire, getting in a woman's way. By dang, if there's one thing I can't stand it's a shiftless, chair-sitting, tobacco-chewing, whisky-tippling, idle man!"

By night, the Parson, aided by the Widow Cobb, got everyone together at Stocker's cabin, the largest Dutchman's Flat had to offer. There were eighteen men, their wives and larger children, a rough-garbed, work-hardened, discouraged group with scarcely a grubstake to show for the season.

Stocker, big and red-whiskered and stubborn as always, got to his feet and said, "We're not quitters. Not us. This is good soil, better'n White Pine, and not so many mosquitoes. We're sticking here, so don't tell us how green it is over the hill."

Big Betsy said, "I fought to keep us together just as hard as you have, and that's just why I called this meeting. Brother John has got an idee that'll let us stick together and give us the money we need. Winter work, and we can farm through the summer."

"Better'n trapping," John added.

"We got no traps," said Kippen.

Stocker was truculent, but he sat down on a bench and listened. Others expected little to come of it, too, but John explained to them just how it was, drawing a map of the pass, telling about this stretch of proposed road and that, and how each would take a piece of it, some long and some short depending on whether it was easy grade or hard, and build the road, after which it was his to charge toll at a rate of two dollars a ton during the snow, and seventy-five cents at other times, and not just for one year, either, but ever and anon, until maybe a railroad came in, which would be never over *these* mountains.

Young, redheaded, banjo-playing Rusty McCabe, who now had a wife and eight-month-old baby to think about, was the first to claim a share. Kippen, who was pulling stakes anyhow, was next; then Stott and his hulking, dull-appearing, fifteen-year-old son, Veltis. An argument ensued whether Veltis should be allotted a full share. It was left unsettled.

John asked for more volunteers. When none offered, Betsy Cobb arose and stormed at them, saying no worthless, loafing, tobacco-chewing man was going to clutter up *her* kitchen that winter, no, not by a crockful, because *she* was declaring *herself* in on the scheme, and claiming a piece of road.

"What do you aim to do, build snowshed or blast rock?" Shallerbach hooted at her, and she answered:

"Neither. You're all going to dig my road for me, because I'm going to feed ye and provide for ye, and have a warm place for ye when you're tired and sick and discouraged."

Stocker then said he would go, and then Shallerbach, Joey Nelson, and Chinless Wally Snite, while Voss said he would think it over. Voss, after talking to his wife, was on hand to sign up next day, and that evening, George Nealy, who had gone prospecting the summer before, got wind of it and came in with two Chinese laborers and asked for a share.

John estimated that these, perhaps with the help of some of Murphy's teamsters, could do the job. He did not care for Snite, who would probably quit anyhow, and he had disliked Ambrose Stocker ever since Stocker had wanted to hang him over on the I-de-ho side, but still and all it was a tolerable group.

It took a couple of days to get the outfits together, and then one more when Kippen and Shallerbach came over from Shako Gulch with a two-horse scraper that required some blacksmithing, but finally they set out, in wagons loaded with camp stuff, spuds, and dry beans, the entire harvest for some of them, with extra horses, mules and oxen coming up in a remuda under the charge of Veltis Stott.

The journey by road required four days. It was evening when they made the last weary pull through Stumptown to the grassy, cirquelike area they had chosen for the main camp. A tent was there, but it was empty, and a note was pinned to the flap, signed by Buck Pelton, saying he had gone to Benton to close the deal for the Frying Pan outfit and would be back Tuesday. Tuesday was the day before. Buck had been delayed.

Comanche John's farmers went to work cutting and skidding logs for shanties, and with that work under way, he rode the high country up and back, first in a general reconnaissance, and next with a square and plumb-bob sighting outfit, surveying the road. After mapping it, he divided it into ten segments, some long and some short, depending on the terrain and on the sheds and trestles that had to be built and trying to figure in the amount of snow that would have to be cleared later on. By then the cabins were far enough along for shelter, and Buck was in from Fort Benton with the vanguard of the Frying Pan freight outfit.

"Where's Murphy?" John asked, noticing the wheel-sprung wagons and the gaunt state of the mules.

Buck did not try to hide his fatigue or his disgust. "In at Jackass, drunk."

Big Betsy Cobb came around to say, "I don't think we should be forming partnerships with a drunken man."

John said, "Sister Cobb, just so his mules are sober, that's all I ask."

John offered to divide the road by lot, or he offered it to their compromise, except that the bottom stretch of half a mile belonged to the Widow Cobb, and that would have to be finished first, as a co-operative venture, in order to get supplies to the upper slope. They decided to go over the ground first, and after a lengthy powwow, Stocker took the long mile-and-a-quarter stretch up from the Widow's; with Kippen, Stott, and Shallerbach going third-shares on the three segments of grade and snowshed to follow; Nelson and Voss taking the next two; Rusty McCabe, who was good at ax work, taking a quarter-mile bridge and snowshed piece; George Nealy some steep grade and fill; and Wally Snite, after a great deal of whining and procrastinating, choosing and rejecting two other segments, finally settling on the 200-yard trestle because it was shortest. This left a bit at the top which John had originally added to the trestle, but was left off to placate Snite. They decided to call it half a share, and give it to Veltis Stott.

While all this was going on, Buck had his trouble with Murphy's teamsters. Many of them had gone a month without pay, and almost to the man they looked at the towering Chilkao and pronounced the whole project to be crazy. With nothing to do, they spent what money they had for whisky and traded all they owned for more, and all the while Murphy was in Jackass City, as drunk as any of them.

Buck finally got Murphy to camp and kept him locked up until he was sober. Murphy emerged repentant. He needed a jug to sober up on, but when that was done, heaven be his judge, he was off the stuff for good. Murphy just wished that somebody had a pledge so he could sign it. He stood outside and said it in a loud voice so everybody in the clearing could hear him, yes, he was off liquor for good, and if anybody found him drunk again he just hoped they'd hit him with a shovel, and beat in his head with it, and then use it to dig a hole and bury him.

He got money from Buck to pay off his teamsters. It cost almost $900. Then he got more money for supplies, and rode away, straight past all the saloons and fancy houses in Jackass City, and he spent it, every cent, for stock feed at a ranch in Deer Lodge. And when he got back he insisted that everybody walk up and smell his breath and see that there was no taint of whisky on it.

Murphy's freight outfit, lying idle, was quickly eating its way through Buck's slender capital. Murphy got a job hauling flour from the mill at Hell Gate. He put other wagons to hauling horn silver ore from the Potosi mine at Lucky Camp over to Fall Creek, where two Mexicans had set up a *patio*. The Potosi owners were broke and paid off in corporate stock, which John declared to be worthless, but which Buck took and sold at a 25% profit to a German hardware merchant in Ruby. Fifteen years later that same block of Potosi would have made him moderately wealthy, for the $10 par stock, which he took at $5, and later sold for $6.25, brought $525.00 a share on the St. Louis mining board. But of this, in 1865, Buck had no anticipation, and the $6.25 price elated everyone.

In the meantime, Betsy Cobb's section of switchback road was completed and the men moved on, each to his own section. Stocker, a Herculean laborer, with the help of a good team and plow, dug out his section of road and shoveled and scraped it level, finishing it in eight days. Above him, Shallerbach, Stott, and Kippen had run into tough going through timber and slide rock around a bald-faced flank of mountain that time after time required drilling and blasting. Kippen decided to quit. He sold his share to Stocker for five dollars and a saddle horse and departed for Last Chance. Now, with Stocker on the job, the tempo increased; he kept them going every daylight hour, and they worked by the light of pitch torches far into the night. Nelson and Voss made headway, and on the next piece McCabe had built a chute and had spent all his time getting out timbers and logging for his snowsheds. He sold a horse and used the money to employ an Indian helper. As yet he had not built an inch of road, and as his segment was cut by a very deep gully, nothing more than a pack-horse could be taken to the sections farther up. Nealy and Turner complained bitterly of this state of affairs until Comanche John sent a crew of Murphy's skinners and roustabouts above to put in a bridge and dig out the main portions of the road.

At the very summit, meanwhile, Veltis Stott surprised everyone. Left to his own resources, with the others predicting that they would have to do the job for him, and that it would teach him not to cut off a man's chew before he could spit, Veltis did what he could with hand tools, and then walked down the other side half a mile to the new shaft building of the L & M's Carlotta Mine, where he pointed out to the superintendent that his road could be used to advantage in bringing mine timbers in from the south side. He then borrowed what he needed, including a team of drillers when the Carlotta's shaft was flooded by a broken steam pump. As a result, he finished almost as soon as Stocker, then, refusing to work on the lower sections of road for just his board and keep, he got a job underground on the Carlotta's No. 2 tunnel swinging a muck stick at $6 a day.

It was now getting on toward November, and the road had to be finished. The lower three-fourths contained many bad stretches, but these could be fixed later on, even with snow on the ground. A try-out wagon, heavy-loaded, had no trouble until it reached Nealy's, where a sharp switchback held by cribbing and rock fill proved too narrow to swing the six-mule team and wagon, and had to be widened. McCabe's snowsheds were still not built, although most of the timber was down, but they could wait. With luck, the heavy snow would not come until mid-December. With more luck they could even get by without snowsheds, for the deep accumulations could be trenched, and later the trenches covered over with poles, and then with new snow to make a tunnel. The thing really barring them was the trestle which Wally Snite had chosen to build because it was the shortest piece, and it looked to him like the easiest.

Snite had dug some footings and skidded about sixty pieces of timber. A series of misfortunes had befallen him: he had cut his foot with an ax; he had been ill with the mountain complaint; his grub had been raided by skunks; one horse went lame, and while he was tending to it, his other horse strayed. Out of grub, he went hunting, got lost, and wandered without food for two days.

The grub situation was particularly galling to Snite. There were the others, most of them close enough so they could ride to the Widow's for one hot meal a day, but here he was, left high and cold with ten thousand skunks, so he had to hang his grub by wires on the limbs of trees; and furthermore he had been shim-shammed into taking the poorest section of road, and nobody would lift a finger to help him; all the others had somebody to help *them*—a partner or a couple of Chinymen—but not him. Why, even that Stott kid had 'em helping him, men bringing equipment over from the mines, and him so dumb he didn't know enough to pour water out of a wet boot. And when, in spite of his luck, he *did* get some timber out and start to place it, and build the trestle, who should come but that black-whiskered scoundrel named Smith, who really wasn't Smith at all, but a road agent, wanted by the law, to tell him he wasn't doing it right, and would have to do it over. Well, Snite said, he'd show them a thing or two, all of them, he'd just sit there, and not lift a finger, and maybe they'd find out he was some important after all.

A meeting was held at the cookhouse. At Stocker's suggestion, Snite's segment was declared forfeit, the others taking it on equal shares. Snite screamed for them to go to the devil. He rode away to Jackass City promising to "see someone," for they'd mighty soon find out where there was a law in the country, and it would prevent them taking a man's property away from him, the same property he'd slaved his fingers to the bone for, because he had *title*, he had a paper signed by Buck Pelton, and it was a *deed*, according to law.

He saw a lawyer, and be damned if it wasn't fat Judge Harrison, the same Judge Harrison who had tried to hang Comanche John in New Boston, and who now had been brought to Jackass City by Hames just to make sure he got justice in the courts. Harrison was driven out in a wagon by a Negro coachman in uniform, the same Negro who ran the feed stable, and who operated this wagon as a hack on the side. Harrison had a notice signed by Ox Miller, president of the Jackass and Gold Run Miners' meeting, filled with ink blots and whereases, saying the road was closed by injunction. He tacked up the notice and rode back. The road wasn't closed, though, because wagons were running over it, and Comanche John, arriving that night, used the notice for target practice. Anyhow, they had greater worries. Frying Pan Murphy was drunk again, he had taken with him the payroll, and the skinners were threatening to quit. One of the mules died. On the day following another died, and on the third, two more.

In Jackass City, word got to Murphy that his mules were dying. He sobered enough to mount a horse and came out with a vet, or a man who said he was a vet, who thumped around a couple of stiffened carcasses and pronounced them dead of poison hemp. When it was pointed out that the plant was unknown in that particular locality, the vet looked superior and departed. Murphy, beset by his unpaid teamsters, also made haste to leave.

"Poison hemp!" Comanche John said. "Waal,

maybe, but I'll wager it came from our old pard, Hames."

They posted guards. Comanche John had a suspicion that guards would be useless. Hames probably had someone right in camp. So that night John posted himself uphill from the corrals, in the deep blackness of spruce timber, and made himself comfortable for a long vigil. There was no moon, but an edging of new snow around about made it light enough to see after a fashion. And he could hear, Comanche had hearing like prowling catamount.

He waited minutes, and hours crept past. It was cold, below freezing, and he had little enough on. By grab, if he wedded the Widow Cobb, *if* he did, the first thing he'd have her make would be some red, hand-knit, wool underwear, thick and scratchy, the kind you sewed yourself into and didn't come out of until April. John's present underwear was as full of holes as a harness, and he didn't have socks, even— only those long-cut strips of wool wrapped around his feet, mummy-style, and they were always gee-hawing, making holes one place and lumps in another.

Suddenly he alerted himself. Someone was coming, and not up the trail from Jackass, but quietly, through the timber, on a deer track directly beneath him.

He waited; he waited for what seemed to be a long time, then he heard a low whistle, and an answering whistle. A shadow moved from behind the cookhouse, a silhouette, tall, with an easy shoulder movement that he recognized. It was Buck Pelton.

"Hello!" he heard Buck say in his husky, quiet voice.

A girl answered—Nettie Bowden.

They'd had it planned to meet; they'd been meeting before; it was all plain to John now. It explained Buck's peculiar night absences, and the way of him when he came in, the drunk-without-likker way of a man in love.

John chuckled to himself. "*Her.* And right from under Hames's nose."

They were in the darkness below him, and were talking quietly; he could hear the notes of their voices without catching any of their actual words. He wanted to hear—not because he was snoopy, but just because he wanted to. So he got closer, sliding down through soft, damp forest cover in time to hear her say that she was certain of it, that her father and Hames were buying Murphy out.

"Murphy can't sell," Buck said. "We own two-thirds of his outfit."

She said, "All I'm telling you is what I heard Dad say. Murphy is selling. They're closing the deal day after tomorrow."

"Why are they waiting?"

"He wants cash. Hames has to wait for his payroll to come up from Salt Lake."

"Where's Murphy now?"

"I don't know."

"We'll have to find him."

They moved away, still talking. John knew that they wouldn't find Murphy. It was too late to do anything about Murphy. Hames would see to *that*. Hames would have Murphy well under cover

CHAPTER NINETEEN

COMANCHE JOHN had a plan of his own. He put up a snack without disturbing Betsy Cobb, and rode off down the gulch and across the ridge, southward. At dawn he was at the creek where he had first met Buck Pelton.

"What a coach robber *that* lad was," he reminated. "No training. Breed is dying out, gitting hung. Trains taking over the old routes. Trains—there's the real death of the coach robber."

By grab, if there was one thing Comanche John despised it was a banging, clanging, stinking train. That's one reason he headed into Montana. They'd never get a train into that territory, that was a certainty, and if they *did*, they'd never get it back out again.

The sun warmed him. He was in no hurry. He had all day and most of the next. He napped on a hillside. He rode on, past Bentley's, and got ready to spend the night in the open, building a bitty lean-to by notching spruce saplings and bending them over and weighting their tips with rocks. It was snug underneath on a bed of boughs, with the soft twigs of the saplings billowing over him. By grab, this was fine. This was really living.

He lay thinking more about railroads, and how they ruined the country. Well, the railroads had come, but they'd go again, yes, they would, after their usefulness was spent, after the mines were worked out and there was no more payload for 'em to haul. He'd listened to the speeches down in Coloraydo when that branch from the U.P. was building, about how the railroad would bring in the farmers, and how the farm things would keep the rails humming, but it was all plain foolishness, lifting themselves by their own bootstraps, the weakness of it being who'd buy the farm stuff after the gold was gone? What'd they pay for it with? With more farm stuff, or with enjine smoke? Oh, yes, John had listened to a lot of big talk in his day, but most of it didn't stand up to the clear thinking of a man out under the stars beneath a spruce lean-to.

In the morning he reached Brass Kettle Creek. He was out of the mountains now, on a sagebrush flat between hills.

He sighted a bridge. That was the spot he'd figured on. He watched a freight outfit move from sight. It left the flat empty as far as his eye could see.

He inspected the bridge. It was made of heavy logs laid crosswise to traffic resting on even heavier logs set in the opposite banks. Traffic had worn down the approaches on both sides, leaving deep holes in the gumbo earth which had been filled in with stones—a rough job.

He removed some stones. He did not take out all of

them, just enough to make a hole that would loosen the coach driver's teeth when he hit it, but not enough to stop his vehicle entirely. He decided to mask himself, fixing a kerchief beneath the band of his hat so it could be pulled down when needed. He left his gunpowder pony back in the bushes, reins around the saddle horn, so he could follow. After that, there was nothing to do but wait. In half an hour he sighted the dust drift of the approaching coach.

He got down and crouched ankle deep in the creek, with cold water slowly finding its way through the seams of his jackboots. Around the projecting end logs of the bridge he could see without being seen.

He wondered if Sanchez would be riding shotgun again, or if his arm had mended. He rather hoped it would be Sanchez, just for the fun of it, and it was. There he sat, hunched over a trifle, that old snaky look about him, a shotgun clamped between his knees, his pistol hitched high to make riding easier.

The coach slowed not a quarter wheel turn as it careened toward the bridge. He had a brief view of the undersides of hoofs and the bellies of horses, then the wheels hit with a bang that loosened every dowel and joint in the coach.

The driver cursed. The rear wheels dropped and came up again. The coach lurched almost off the bridge. Comanche John pulled himself up, slowed by his water-filled boots, paused at a crouch. The side of the coach was over him; people were there; they could have looked down and seen him, they could have touched him, but the unexpected impact was like being belted over the skull. They weren't in condition to see anyone. The rear wheel barely missed him. He stood and grabbed the luggage carrier, pulled himself up, climbed to the hurricane.

The driver, standing, was filling the air with curses for the sodbusters and punkin-rollers whom he blamed for the state of the bridge. Sanchez sat tight, clutching the iron seat rail, apparently still a trifle groggy from the impact.

John, on hands and knees, pulled the kerchief over his face. He drew his right-hand Navy and said, "Covered!"

He spoke softly so his voice would not be heard inside the coach, but it reached the driver and Sanchez, and they stiffened to its tone.

"No, don't look around. Keep your eyes on the road and your minds on staying alive."

"Where the devil did *you* come from?" shouted the driver.

"I be first cousin to the eagle and brother to the hawk, but don't ask me the secrets of my clan. The point is, I'm robbing this stagecoach. I'm after the Hames payroll; it's here; it was put aboard in Salt Lake, and if ye want to know the exact amount I could give ye that, too."

He said all this, trying to disguise his voice, but just the same knowing he'd be recognized by Sanchez, who sat with his shoulders pulled in, looking straight ahead, the rifle still clamped between his knees. A bandage around his right forearm was a reminder of that other encounter, but he could use the hand, he was using it to grip the barrel of the rifle.

John poked his Navy against Sanchez's spine. "Git up."

Sanchez did so, straightening his legs, propping himself with the backs of his legs against the seat.

"Loosen your gun belt. Thar. Let it fall. Good. That's first rate. That's top riffle. I can see ye been robbed before. Know better'n to cause trouble when you're up agin' a man that knows his business. Just let the rifle go. It'll lean. Step over it. Thar. That's fine. By grab, you've mastered the art of staying alive in the wild Nor'west. Now turn, face the outside, jump!"

For the first time Sanchez hesitated, and for the first time he looked. John had anticipated that, and anticipated the dive that he might make for him; but Sanchez didn't have the chance, for John's right jackboot shot out, catching him in the belly, doubling him, sending him sprawling to the ground in waist-high sagebrush.

The dry sage raised a billow of gray dust as the coach rolled on.

"Man overboard!" a passenger bellowed, leaning out of the window, trying to get the driver's attention. "Hey, somebody fell off the top."

"Don't answer," said Comanche John.

The passenger leaned farther out and kept shouting and pointing at Sanchez, who by now was on his feet, just standing there, watching.

"You lost a man overboard!"

The passenger stopped suddenly as he looked into the muzzle of Comanche John's Navy.

"It war his destination," John said politely, "but this be a scheduled coach, and wayside passengers git off on the fly. Reggylations. And don't go to yawping agin' 'em or I'll punch your ticket for ye, and I'll do it with a thirty-six-caliber hole, and I'll do it without taking it out of your breast pocket."

John heard no more from inside the coach. He settled back. He enjoyed the ride, chawing, looking at the scenery which actually wasn't so much, only the sage-and-jackpine-covered hills with roundish, heaped-up lava rocks forming some narrows out ahead. That would be the place—the narrows. He could stop there and wait for his horse, and keep watch both ways, and in case of trouble he could fight off a whole posse.

He propped his boots up to let some of the water run out, he even hummed a tune, but not the Comanche John tune, for it might have hinted who he was.

"Well?" cried the driver, stiff at the edge of the seat.

"No hurry. We'll heave-to in the rocks. I'll stay fixed and you dump off the money chest." He was keeping watch of the driver without seeming to, and a slight movement of the fellow's mouth told him something. Of course it wouldn't be the main strongbox—Hames would know better. Hames would be too foxy. "The *private* chest. The small one, the hid one." He noted with satisfaction that he'd hit on it. He chuckled. At New Boston Hackven had shown him where Hames hid the gold. "Ye shouldn't think to fool me. Didn't I tell ye it was aboard? And *whar* it'd *come* aboard? Might be no end to the things I know. I want Hames's private pay money, no more, no less, and it'd be unhealthy to try to trick me."

The driver was very jittery. "I'll not try to trick you." And John knew that he wouldn't.

They stopped amid red-brown rocks that radiated the sun, and the driver, reaching inside around the passengers, opened the secret compartment and got out a plain satchel. It was locked, so John slit the leather with his bowie, reached in, and inspected the packets of money. Union money, those down-and-out greenbacks, the kind ye should spend fast before old Robbie Lee took Washington and started stabling his horses in the soo-preme court, and put the government printing office to making handbills for all the runaway slaves that the abolitionists had spirited away from the honest property owners of the South. It amazed him that Frying Pan Murphy would want this sort of stuff in payment for the mules and wagons of his freight line. Well, he wouldn't get it, not this money, because John had it.

He drew the money out, a packet at a time, and stuffed it inside his shirt, cinching up his belt so it wouldn't leak out down his pants legs. Finished, he climbed to one of the outjutting rocks.

"Now git," he said. "Drive and keep driving."

Half an hour later his pony was there, coming at John's whistle to get a handful of brown sugar, and John rode back toward Jackass.

He arrived late. A crowd was on the street, most of them gathered near Judge Harrison's law office, so he guessed that the coach had arrived, the robbery had been reported, and the miners' meeting had convened.

He decided to make no display of himself. He left the street, descending to the safety of the deep placer

cut. The sluices, miles of dripping plank troughs, tonight ran clear water with everyone, even the Chinese
laborers, up listening to the speeches.

Somebody was saying that somebody ought to build
a gallows, and build it *now,* so it'd be ready, because
Comanche John would be up there, at the freight
camp, on the other side of Stumptown, and they ought
to burn it out, and hang some of the others, too, because it was a nest of thieves, and anybody but a fool
could see it was a blind, that freight road, over country so steep it'd maroon a goat, and snow so deep later
on you couldn't log-pull a toboggan over it.

Then another man got up to have his say. He was in
favor of hanging Comanche John, too, but talk
wouldn't do it. No, he thought they ought to *catch* Comanche first and hang him afterward. That didn't set
well with the previous speakers, who started to heckle
him, and that made him mad. He was red-freckled
and redheaded and undersized, and the kind who got
really mad. Yes, he shouted back at them, he'd been in
Idaho and knew about the Comanche, all the places
they'd *claimed* to hang him, and *tried* to hang him,
and if they *did* catch him they'd better hang him with
a rough rope, because he had the slipperiest Adam's
apple this side of Pike County, Missouri, and when
they got him hung they'd better cement him in his
grave, and roll eighteen ton of grandiorite porphyry
on his chest, and then not brag a word for ten days
and ten nights because the old Comanche was the
type that wriggled through a small hole.

"Yipee!" whispered John, slapping the legs of his
homespuns, barely restraining the impulse to go right
up there and shake that man's hand. "That's me, I'm a
ring-tailed ripper from the Rawhide Mountains, and
I'm harder to hold than the weasel that fell in the soap
bucket."

Ox Miller then charged back to the platform, braying about the honor of the territory. "Ladies and gentlemen," Ox said, although the only "ladies" present
were some of the girls leaning from the second-story

windows of the New Orleans dance hall across the street. "Ladies and gentlemen, I speak to you of the honor of the territory, and of Jackass City, the future hub of transportation of the entire Nor'west, and especially of the man who is putting her there, Mr. Lawford Hames, and how he's been robbed and victimized and driven to the end of his patience, and how something should ought to be done about it. Well, I say something *will* be done about it. We'll go up there to that den of thieves called Stumptown, and *get* Comanche John, and *hang* him, and as for me, I'm willing to do it as a civic deed, and no thought to the reward. Yes, as for the money, I'm willing to contribute my share to the city, and it can be used to buy things to enhance the town—gas lights on iron posts, and a water system, and a fire engine, and a monument to George Washington, the father of our country—"

"Hold on, Ox," somebody shouted. "How much ree-ward they got up for that road agent?"

"Plenty. Here, and I-de-ho, and Californy—just plenty. And I say we should write letters this very night informing 'em we've *hung* Comanche John, and the rewards are due, and payable as of this date, and if they try to renege they'll be sued."

Such foolishness was too much for Comanche John's stomach, so he rode on, staying to the shadow until he saw the lights of Stumptown.

Stumptown looked nothing like it had a month or two before. In anticipation of its future eminence as the jumping-off place to Windigo Pass, it had grown from its first clutch of cabins to a town of two hundred, with a dozen keg-and-tincup saloons, a couple of stores, and a dance hall with a temporary canvas roof. Tonight everyone was awake, and the word of John's arrival raced along the street.

He stopped as Fred Bentloss, the storekeeper, townsite promoter, and unofficial mayor came toward him.

"You have your crust, Smith, riding up here like this with all that ruckus going on in Jackass. Did you know they intend to hang you? You'll get us all in trouble."

"I do feel sorry for ye," John said with poor temper, getting one leg around the bulge of his saddle for comfort. "I'll tell ye something else they plan on, and that's burning ye out, all of ye, the whole damn town. Can't ye *see?* I'm Comanche John, so they say, and *why?* What's the real reason? I'll tell ye—to give 'em an excuse, wreck the town, wreck the road, make Jackass City the freight hub instead of Stumptown."

This put a new light on it. "They're not burning my place down," one of the saloonkeepers bellowed. "I got *three hundred dollars* invested in my place, and they'll be plenty of Jackassers carrying bullet lead before *I* let 'em set fire to it."

Someone else said he'd been there, and he'd heard talk about burning the town, that Ox Miller himself had called it a den of thieves.

Stumptown was really excited now, arming and barricading itself. Bentloss tried to take command, but before he could bring any sort of order a boy rode from the direction of Jackass, quirting his pony, shouting, "They're coming, they're coming. There must be five hundred of 'em."

Two-thirds of that number there might have been, but fortunately most of them had just come to see the hanging. Ox Miller, tramping along in the lead, drew up when he saw the log barricade they'd hastily thrown across the road.

"Stand back," Bentloss called out. "You're not burning Stumptown."

A warning gun cracked, adding point to his words. Ox dived for cover and the men behind him scattered. Someone from the Jackass crowd fired back, and then guns let go from everywhere.

When things quieted they could hear Ox bellowing, "Bentloss? Hear me, Bentloss, you taking responsibility for sheltering an outlaw?"

"You're not burning us out."

"We got no idea of burning ye out."

But the firing commenced again. Ox retreated, recognizing the futility of argument. Dawn came, gray at first, and then with a touch of color around the high peaks. With daylight, it was all over. The only casualty was Lou Haffey, owner of the Michigan saloon, who lay on his pine bar with a bullet through both legs. As for Comanche John, he had long since ridden to Betsy Cobb's for breakfast.

CHAPTER TWENTY

"LANK," Betsy Cobb muttered, stopping her work now and then to look at him as he sat there. "Hungry as a ranging wolf. You been on a wolf's business, too, more'n likely."

Talking from the only part of his mouth not full, Comanche John said, "I been on company business o' confidential nature, Sister Cobb, convincing Frying Pan Murphy he shouldn't sell out to Hames."

Buck Pelton came through the door behind him and asked, "How did you know about Murphy and Hames?"

"I be an old woolly-wolf; I sniff things in the air."

Buck laughed and sat down across from him and watched him load his mouth with fat side and griddle-cake. "I hear that Hames can't raise the money."

"Saddened to hear it. Whar is Murphy now?"

"I don't know."

"Under lock, I'll wager, or kept too drunk to move. So be it. Hames is welcome to him. If thar's one thing the Widda Cobb and me can't stand it's a whisky-drinking man."

John insisted on paying all the teamsters double wages. He was very free with greenbacks. Dissatisfied with progress on the trestle, he hired men at half again more than the prevailing wage. On the third day after the Battle of Stumptown, he awoke to find a blizzard licking around the mountain, drifting snow across Mc-

Cabe's uncompleted snowshed, but the work went on, with men quitting and John raising wages to get them on again, for it was November, and the first 200 tons of contract time freight would be due in Ruby by the fifteenth.

"We'll make it," Comanche John said, coming down from the pass after a day and a night without sleep, stamping wet snow on the Widow's floor, rubbing his ears, which were discolored from the cold. "We'll git the freight over. By the way, whar *is* the freight?"

Buck was seeing about the freight. It was piling up at the Willard & Sankey warehouse in Jackass City, but Ox Miller, with fifty blank warrants, was waiting to arrest the first "Stumptown rebel" who came to claim it.

Buck returned, having succeeded in escaping arrest, and rode straight on over the pass to see the London & Montana people about it. He returned with a note from Hutton, addressed to Willard & Sankey, threatening to terminate all company business with that firm, whereupon the resident manager bustled around among the Jackass City business concerns, pulling enough strings to get Ox to rescind his order, and the first wagons were loaded without incident.

Now they waited for the trestle to be finished. Temporary plank, laid across, allowed the passage of an empty wagon. That night, by torchlight, the first four payload wagons started up the pass. It still snowed, but crews went ahead, keeping the way cleared. By morning they were at Nealy's, where a dirt slide held them up. It was cleared, and they rolled on, beneath snowsheds, roofed with pine-pole logging, and already, in places, drifted over, forming tunnels. The trestle workmen, catching sight of them, raised a cheer: "Hip-hip-hooray!" In the midst of this, no one paid any attention to the three men who were walking across the trestle from the Ruby side. Each of these carried a brace of Navies, and the big fellow in the lead had a sawed-off double gun for good measure.

Dillworth was shouting, "Get back to pegging plank

and stop hootin' your heads off," but when the first workman started back he found himself stopped against the muzzle of the double gun.

"No, you don't," the man said, and he meant it. The man was Moose Petley. Back of him were Sanchez and Billy Step-and-a-Half, who had recently arrived from New Boston.

Stocker cried, "What goes on there?" and drew up, recognizing him. "Why, you're Moose Petley!"

"Yes, you're damn right I'm Moose Petley, and no, you didn't kill me on the Big Hole; *murder* me, I should say, ingratitude if I ever seen it, after the way I fought your Injuns and showed you the trail. Well, we're on the other side of the gun today, and this is legal, because I'm *Deppity* Petley, duly sworn. And that's Deppity Sanchez, and Deppity Step-and-a-Half, and we got plenty more, uphill and all around, so you see what you're up against."

"What do you want?"

"I got a writ of attachment for this bridge."

"Who from?"

Moose, holding the sawed-off with an elbow and one hand, drew a paper from the pocket of his curly-buffalo coat and, holding it upside down, announced, "Whereas and to wit, this section of road, bein' known as the Sky-High Trestle, belonging truly to Mr. Walter J. Snite, a freeholdin' citizen of this republic, is hereby seized and appropriated for the benefit of him and his heirs forever."

"Who signed it?" a man jeered. "Was it Lawford Hames, or that San Francisco millionaire that's backing him?"

"The *judge* signed it. There's his name."

Nealy had come up around the crowd, against the inner bank where, for a distance, the road had been blasted from the mountainside. In his hands was a newfangled German needlefire rifle. He stepped out, away from the others, surprising Moose with the aimed gun.

"Now, git or you're a dead man!" Nealy shouted.

A gun cracked from above, and Nealy went down, head and shoulders first, across the steep side of the road. He slid for ten or twelve feet, and might have gone over the cliff farther down, but he was caught by jack spruce and juniper, and there he lay, apparently not breathing.

For the space of one or two seconds everyone seemed stunned by the shot. Then they milled, looking for cover. The cry of "Ambush!" went up. A puff of gunsmoke hung over stunted spruce at the rim of the cliff.

Someone fired from the road. A bullet hit rock and screeched. There were more shots from above. One of the workmen fell, and got up and ran, bent and staggering, and fell, and got up again, and someone grabbed him and dragged him to cover.

Moose Petley and his two companions were momentarily forgotten, and they lost no time getting down off the trestle. They were beneath, sliding the steep rock, using pilings and brace timbers to check their descent, and for protection, too.

"Get Nealy!" Stott cried, and when no one moved he went himself, pushing away those who tried to stop him.

Stott was all by himself in the road. A bullet whanged down, showering stone and snow between his boots. He flattened himself against the cut-away bank and shouted, "Moose, stop your guns, let me get that wounded man, where's your Christian mercy?"

Moose answered, "I'll show Nealy the same brand of Christian mercy he'd have shown me if we hadn't got him first."

Nealy, in the meantime, had shaken off bullet shock and rolled over. He got to hands and knees. He made it to the road. Sanchez had crawled around, uphill, and lifted his pistol to fire, but Shallerbach saw him and poked his old 50-caliber Jaeger rifle over a log, aimed, and pulled the trigger, all in one movement. Sanchez fired wildly; the impact of the Jaeger slug knocked him over on his back; he had enough left to spring to his feet, then his legs buckled and he gave the impression of springing head foremost to the trestle; he hit one timber and another, his weight knocking one of the braces loose, and ended, sliding through rock and snow almost at Moose Petley's feet where he lay without moving.

"Get 'em, go get 'em!" Moose was bellowing to his men on the cliff above. "Blow 'em back to Stumptown," he shouted without once showing so much as a sleeve of his curly-buffalo coat.

Stott in the meantime had dragged Nealy to cover. He was not badly hurt. Other rifles from above drove the road builders back, first to the protection of Nealy's bridge, and then to a snowshed. From there, some of them doubled back along the mountain. Both sides holed up, with neither in actual control of the trestle.

It was evening when word of the battle reached Comanche John in Stumptown. He went from saloon to cabin to barbershop trying to raise a force of men, but he found only three who would join him, and one of those was a boy of fifteen who was soon dragged home by an irate mother. John then looked for Buck Pelton. Someone had seen him walking to Betsy Cobb's. Betsy was alone and in such a state as John had never before seen her.

"She'll kill him, she'll kill him," Betsy was saying.

"Who'll kill who? Sit down, woman, and stop waving that old horse pistol. Who'll kill who?"

"That girl, she was here with a gun, and it was cocked, and it was loaded. Do you think I'd have let her threaten him if it hadn't been—"

"What girl? Nettie Bowden?"

Betsy cried, "She's the one, that vixen, that devil—"

"*Her?* That pretty, sweet—"

"She's a young devil with skirts on," said Betsy. "She's incarnate. The Good Book warns us of her kind."

He couldn't believe it. "She after Buck with a gun?"

"She walked him out of here at the point of a pistol, with the hammer drawn back, and not three minute ago. Oh, I been in a state. I didn't know what to do. Buck told me to sit right here or—"

"What'd she want?"

"Claimed we had her paw, old Bowden, a prisoner, a hostage, that old moneybags, that wicked old San Francisco skinflint—"

"Whar'd they go?"

"How do I know? Toward Jackass, I suppose."

"Afoot?"

"Horseback. It's four mile—o' course they're horseback."

Comanche John rode off at a gallop, through Stumptown, down the freight road, among the cabins which were interspersed with clumps of timber where one settlement frayed out to meet the other.

It was dark here, with only an occasional cabin window to light his way. The houses became more numerous. This was Jackass City. He would have to move more carefully. Behind him, a man in a cabin door stood with a blue-flaming match. It gave him a start, the quick burst of its flame, like the flame of gunpowder, but the man was only lighting his pipe.

He was close onto the Jackass business district and about ready to turn back when he looked up a steep street terminating against a cut-bank, and there they were.

"Ho, thar!" he said.

She recognized him. He saw the blued shine of gunmetal in her hand. She tried to watch both ways and was plainly at a loss where to point the gun.

"I mean ye no harm," said Comanche John. "And you're wrong about the lad, too." He took off his black slouch hat and held it over his breast in a posture of sincerity. "We got no idee what could have happened to your pa."

She cried, "Perhaps you'll tell me I'm wrong when I say you used the information *he* got from me," she pointed to Buck, "and used it to intercept Hames's payroll. That was the start of Dad's trouble—"

"Buck had nothing to do with robbing that coach. I

robbed it myself. It war my own idee. I was uphill that very night, hearing every word ye said. So he didn't abuse your confidence. But as for holding your paw a hostage, why that ain't our style."

"I have a letter signed by you—"

"By *me?* Gal, I can't even read and write, except for the things wrote on a pack of playing cyards, and that's the handwriting of the devil, I been told."

She had already put the gun down. It was plain that she was relieved to have Buck Pelton absolved from blame. She was so relieved that she had no ire left for Comanche John.

"Oh, Buck!" she said, almost in tears.

He turned his horse and rode close to her; they sat so close that their knees touched; he put an arm around her.

He said, "Now tell me what happened—what really happened."

"I think they had a quarrel—Dad and Hames. It was about the mules and some other things. I think Dad threatened to pull out of the partnership. It would have broken Hames. He needs money. He claimed the L and M was holding back on their freight, thinking they could get it over your road cheaper. Then Dad disappeared. I just didn't see him any more. I tried to get Ox Miller to look for him. He did—for a while. Then Hames said that Dad was being held prisoner in Stumptown. He said he had a ransom note from Comanche John."

The gunpowder roan moved, and now he had his head up. Comanche John became alert. He turned and started back the trail. He watched for movement, he listened. He was slouched, his shoulders loose, his hands hanging beneath the out-thrust butts of his Navies. He hummed a little tune and spat tobacco juice at the top of a stump.

He could see only the black shadows of cabins, and of pines, and the soft phosphorescence of snow up the mountain.

"Ho-hum," yawned John, so he could be heard at

some distance. "Reckon I'll ride on to the hotel for a drop of civilized likker."

He had no intention of riding to the hotel. Once on the road, he intended to hit for Stumptown at a gallop, but he did not get to the road; a shadow disengaged itself from the shadow of a hut. He kept riding. There were other men, and there was a shine of guns in their hands.

"Halt!" a voice said. "Move and we'll sink ye with lead."

By reflex John had drawn his Navies. He stopped without lifting them. There were men ahead and at both sides and behind. It was a deadfall, and he had ridden into it. *She* had led him into it—that was his first thought. Only how could she, not knowing he would follow? Then he remembered the flame. It was a signal; it was all set up; they had been waiting for this, waiting to grab him the first time he ventured to set foot in Jackass City.

CHAPTER TWENTY-ONE

COMANCHE JOHN opened his hands and let his Navies fall. The gun struck with scarcely a sound on the damp forest cover. He kept riding at a slow jog, saying, "Why, gent'men, what sort o' celebration ye got fixed up for me?"

"You're covered." The voice belonged to Ox Miller. "Hey, Snipe or whatever your name is, come over here. You identify this man for certain as Comanche John?"

The man he called "Snipe" was Wally Snite. He came gangling and weasel-faced to peer at John. Tonight he carried a Navy pistol in one hand. He was a man of importance, and he made the identification, peering from several angles, and with a swagger.

"That's him!" said Snite. "I identify him. He revealed himself as Comanche John over on the Idaho side, hired out to guide a wagon train I was one of the captains of, tried to get us ambushed, *would* have, too, if it hadn't been for Mr. Hames and myself."

"Waal, hoo-raw for Snipe," said John.

"No doubt we got the right man," said Ox. "We got to file signed i-dentification for some of the ree-ward. Now, stay back. Watch for trouble. He's likely to make a run for it."

"Not me," John said. "I aim to live for a year or three."

"You won't live for an hour," said Snite.

Miller said, "Get his guns. You, Snipe, on that side, and Cary, you."

John said, "Ye got me wrong, boys, I carry no metal, it's agin' my religion."

Cary walked up cautiously, and felt for his pistols. "Clean," he said. "Holsters empty."

"Look in his saddle leather."

"He's clean, I tell you."

Buck Pelton came riding down but was kept away by their leveled guns.

"Stay clear, lad," John said. And when Buck commenced to talk rough to Ox Miller: "No, git home!"

"Don't let him go to Stumptown—he'll get a crew together."

"Let him!" Snite said. "Nothing I'd rather have than some of those Stumptown scalps on my saddle."

They bound John's hands in front of him, each wrist with tight wrappings of rope with a swivel knot in the middle so he was able, handcuff-style, to manage his horse.

"Tie his legs, too," Ox said.

Cary answered, "Oh, hell, Ox, there's no point being an idiot. They'll laugh at us, bringing him in like a Ee-gyptian mummy."

Ox resigned the point, but he still didn't like it. He had heard too many stories about John's previous escapes—about the time he got away with a rope still around his neck, and how he'd been buried, but was too tough to die, and had been dug up, in the middle of the night, by his Arapaho sweetheart; but, of course, that one was just plain foolish.

"He's all right," said Snite. "I hope he does try to escape." He pressed the cold muzzle of a pistol to the skin back of John's left ear. "I only hope he *does* try it!"

Ox said *all right,* but they'd better get him to town, no telling what those renegades at Stumptown would try. They'd better get him in and try him and convict him and hang him.

"Bless you," said John, "I knew ye wouldn't hang me without full benefit of the law. And I know ye won't hang me without the supplications of a minister of my own faith, either."

"Where is he?"

The Parson was yonder at Ruby, establishing a freight warehouse by day and holding revivals by night.

Cary said, "We'll give you till midnight—if you're lucky."

They were getting their horses from sheds, from the timber, from below in the placer cut, but no more than a few were gone at once, and always three or four guns were kept aimed at him.

By now, word of his capture had raced along the gulch. Men were in doorways calling it to their neighbors. A foot crowd formed; others hurried to join them. A tall man, very popeyed and lumpy of face, had carried a torch up from the headbox of a sluice, and when they started toward Main Street he placed himself in the lead.

"They got him; they hanging him tonight; it's Comanche John," he shouted.

"They hung him two year ago in Californy and I seen the corpse," someone called.

A boy of twelve or thirteen competed with him, beating a tin pan, shouting, "It's the Comanche, they caught the Comanche."

It soon developed into a full-blown parade with

pans beating and men keeping time, saying, "Hip! Hip! Hip-hup-hip!" as they marched.

"Get a rope," someone shouted. Someone else shouted it, and in a few seconds everyone was shouting it. Standing on the log wall of a half-finished building a man was calling, "Hang him here. Hang him on my premises. I'll pay a hundred dollars, spot cash, to charity, if you hang him on my rooftree."

"By grab," said John without being heard by anyone, "I never knew I was so popular."

"Hundred dollars to *what* charity?" Ox asked.

"To the widows and orphans of the Union army."

"Make it two hundred."

"Two hundred it is."

The lumpy-faced man, still with his torch, headed into the roofless building. "Make way, make way!"

Someone had a rope. It was tossed over the ridgepole. A knot was tied.

"Get a bar'l."

"We don't need a bar'l. We'll hang him off his horse."

John, who found his time shortening unexpectedly, cried, "Hold on! What sort of small-skate camp is this ye got hyar? Don't I git a trial?"

"You already had a trial."

This was a new voice. It was Hames. He wasn't leaving it to anyone else tonight. He had come through the building by the rear and now stood beneath the swinging rope. He stood with his feet set, hands on hips, tall and powerful. He had a brace of Army pistols strapped around the outside of his coat, and he carried his old bullwhip, the butt projecting from his right pocket.

"I warn't here," said John. "How could ye hold a trial?"

"You didn't need to be here. You were tried and convicted."

"By *you*, Hames? I knew ye owned the camp, bragged about owning it, and Ox Miller war just your errand boy."

'You won't start a quarrel here," Hames barked, obviously afraid that he might.

A few of those in the crowd now started saying that he should have a trial, but most of them wanted to see a hanging, and they mobbed in, pushing the horses of prisoner and captors across the corduroy walk to the open-roofed building.

"Every man deserves a word in his own behalf," shouted John.

Cary stopped against the push of the crowd and swung his horse around, making room. "By damn, yes." He used his gun to drive them back. "I say yes, he ought to have his say."

"You gone crazy? Let's hang him while we got him."

"Even a Chinyman should have his say."

"He's going to talk." The word was passed along. "Comanche John is going to make a speech."

Ox Miller saw that this had found favor with the crowd. After all, he was their elected officer, so he stood in the stirrups, cupped his hands, and bawled out, "He's going to talk. Hear ye, he'll have his say. Now quiet down so we can git it over and have our hanging."

The voices died. John cleared his throat. He waited until the last talker had stopped and it was so quiet he could hear the running boots of late-comers thudding the sidewalks.

"Ladies and gent'men," he started, "I stand before ye a guilty man."

His words shocked everybody.

"He admits it!" a man whooped.

"Yes, I admit it. I been a road agent for twenty year; my soul is black with sin and my hands with powder smoke. I been wicked to shame Gomorrah. Behold ye a man that could have been something, only he took the wrong road, chasing after false prophets, and look at him now. Go ahead, look at him. Look at them boots." He shook one of them. "Leak snow. Sole all loose. No socks, even. Just wrappings of flannel. Homespun pants with knees busted out. No underwear, even."

"You don't need warm clothes where you're going, John."

"That's true. I won't, because the ile in my lamp of righteousness is mighty low. That's why I wanted to talk, so I could warn the young, tell 'em not to follow the trail I did. Don't carry more'n one gun. Avoid strong drink and bad companions. But if ye must rob, do it proper, military style, and never spend a poke in the same camp whar ye got it. That's how I operated, and though I'm a goner tonight, I lasted many a mile farther'n most road agents. Yes, I did, and I drop a tear when I think about 'em, all the brave lads, Jimmy Dale, Three-Gun Bob, Whisky Anderson, and a heap more, all under the sod, hyar, I-de-ho, Coloraydo, Cal-iforny."

He paused, thinking, digging at his whiskers with brown fingers on which, by torchlight, the nails stood out white as pieces of chalk. "Plenty gold I took, but I never had the chance to enjoy it. Never even had a chance to spend a lot of it."

"What happened to it, then?" This was the fateful question, but John made no sign, he was waiting for it.

"I'd tell ye that, yes, I would. I'd tell ye whar I put it, only it would do ye no good. That gold would be the ruination of ye. Gold is the root of all evil. It's the root and the branch, too, and it's the apple that blooms on the tree."

A short, thick-bodied man pushed in as close as he could and said, "It's my gold if it came off that Bentley coach in June."

"The Bentley coach?" John hung his head. "I can't look ye in the eye for shame, but I must confess it war me that robbed that coach."

"What'd you do with my gold?"

"Wait." He lifted hands for quiet. "All in due time. I hold nothing back. I'm in a mood to confess. I robbed that coach, I did, and the one in August, too, and I robbed the bullion wagon from Brass Kettle Creek, I forget the date, and the coach to Last Chance at Cliffrock Station. Then thar was the strongbox at Mauch Gulch, and the Bannock coach at Badger Pass, I think June eleventh, and the retort amalgam from Silver Bow, but I lost *that* in a faro game."

John was not through; he went on, enumerating his robberies, all he had heard about, and some he made up, but finally he stopped, saying that wasn't all, he'd forgotten some, and was sorry, but his memory wasn't what it used to be.

"You got all that and still no money for underwear?" asked Cary.

"Alas, it's the truth. I could get the gold but often as not I didn't dare spend it. Dee-tectives made it too dangerous. Them and their assays, know every shipment, kept watch for it. But I had an idee." He said this last in confidence, looking all around as if afraid that some interloper from Ruby or Last Chance might overhear.

"You buried it?" somebody asked.

"No, I didn't. Not exactly. Better idee than that. I took that gold, and brought it here, and dumped it, of night, in the tailings of the mines. Just in certain places, of course, known to me, marked in my mind. I figured I'd come back when the gulch was worked out, everybody moved on, and stake the old ground, and mine it over again. That way I'd be in the clear, a legitimate mining man, a millionaire, or a hundred-thousandaire anyhow. But I'll never do it now. Too late, alas. I'll be hung and beyond mining, ever."

A dozen men were now demanding to know exactly which tailings had been salted. Then two of them got to jangling and almost came to blows over the right to certain tailings heaps, one claiming them because they originated on his claim, the other because he had the ground they were dumped on.

"I paid you seventy-five ounces of gold for the right to dump on your poor-scratch hardpan claim," the one cried in a fury, "and those tails are mine. I own 'em,

I'll fight for 'em, I'll sue you through every court in the territory."

Ox Miller got them apart and said, "We'll settle it in miners' court. Anyhow, what makes you think John picked *your* claim to salt? Center o' town, too risky, he wouldn't go thar. More'n likely he went down the gulch and sprinkled it on mine."

"Ask *him*."

"Yes, where did you dump it?"

"Not all in one place," said John.

"But where? What places?"

"I did it here and thar, by landmark; I'd have to hunt."

"Show us!" they all started shouting.

"Why, I'd be pleased," said John. "Yes, I would, or-dinarily, only it's dark now, and I'd have to wait for morning, and I'm all confessed now, and well, damn it, I sort of had my mind set on getting hung."

Hames, furious that the miners' meeting could con-tain such gullibility, climbed to the unfinished log wall and shouted down, "He's lying, he's hid no gold, he's stalling for time."

"Well enough for you to talk," he was answered. "You got no claim, you don't stand to lose, all you care about is getting rid of a freight competitor."

"That's a lie. I have the good of the community at heart, and the investment I've made goes to prove it."

"Tell me to my face it's a lie."

"I'm telling you to your face."

Ox Miller didn't know what to do. He knew it was a ten-to-one chance that John was lying, but there was that *one* chance, and, damn it, he owned some tailings, too.

He rode back and forth, trying to keep the crowd away, saying, "We'll call a miners' meeting. We'll put it to a vote."

The lumpy-faced man had wedged his torch down between two segments of the corduroy so he could use both hands to gesture with while engaging in the dis-pute. Comanche John let them jostle him closer to

that torch. It was there, so close his pony twitched
from the heat of it on his side. He unstirruped his boot
and held it out, the edge of the sole in the flame. It
was hot on his toes, but he kept wiggling them, and he
stood it until his boot sole commenced to smolder. No
one paid the least attention to him. They were still
arguing. He pulled his foot back, slowly, casually,
without looking, and touched the burning leather to
the side of his horse.

The gunpowder moved as though stung by a bee.
He had no room to run, so he went off the ground at a
sunfishing leap, and John allowed himself to be cata-
pulted over his head to the space between the walk
and the hitchrack.

The horse, bucking and snorting in a small circle,
sent people headlong to save themselves. No one for
those seconds noticed that Comanche John was no
longer on the pony's back. He crawled as fast as he
could go in the partial cover of the walk. There was
Ox Miller on the other side of the hitchrack fighting
his big gray horse with a stiff bridle rein. Comanche
John climbed to the rail, balanced himself for a second,
and leapfrogged across the horse's rump. He was in
the saddle wedged behind Ox. Ox was shouting,
"What the hell," and John got his tied hands over his
head, around him.

Ox fought. His strength would have freed him had
it not been for the ropes on John's wrists, but these
held him like a hoop around a barrel.

"Ya-hoo!" said Comanche John. "What say to a gallop?"

Ox cursed him and ripped from side to side, almost
dumping both of them to the ground. John's hands located a Navy. He managed to draw it. He turned it in-
ward and pressed the barrel to Ox's stomach.

"Got ye covered!"

"You'll never get away," said Ox, his abdomen stiff
at feel of the gun.

"Pull your bowie!"

"What?"

"Bowie!"

Ox drew the knife.

"Blade out."

Ox did that, too, and John, working the rope up once and down once, cut it, and his hands were free.

As the rope parted, Ox was freed, too. He came around with an elbow aimed at the side of John's head, but John, grasping Ox's other Navy, was already over the side.

"Thar he is," cried Ox. "He's yonder by the hitchrack."

Comanche John seized the torch and hurled it as far as he could. He took a long step as a bullet tore slivers from the walk between his feet. He was against the unfinished wall as a second bullet thudded deep into a log.

"Hyar I am," he whooped. "I'm half catamount and half grizzly b'ar, and the other half of me is horned lizard, too tough to eat and to ornery to die." He climbed the wall. The swinging noose almost hit him in the face. Wally Snite, a loose-jointed scarecrow clutching a gun, had been trying to find a hiding place. He saw John and tried to turn. John kicked him in the stomach and sent him sprawling. He got up. He had dropped his gun. He saw Hames through the unfinished doorway. He reeled out and tried to catch hold of Hames's jacket and tell him John was there, somewhere along that shadowy wall. Hames turned, furious at the escape, and drove the barrel of his gun to the side of Snite's head.

Snite went down like a dead man. Men trampled him.

"There he goes!" said Hackven.

John hit him with a blast from his left-hand Navy, dropping him in his tracks.

"Whoop-a-raw!" he bellowed. "I'm a ring-tailed ripper from the Rawhide Mountains and I've kilt more men than the seven-year plague." He did a dance in his jackboots and fired through the window and door openings to keep them back. "I've shot men sidewise and I shot 'em endwise, and I stacked 'em up like cordwood at the steamboat landing, so stand aside and give me room because this is my choice of a place to start a cemetery."

He crawled through one of the side window holes. He dropped to damp earth on hands and knees. He crawled. He got up and ran, following a narrow passage between the unfinished building and a saloon next door. He could have gone on, up a zigzag path to the next street, but they would expect him to do that. He crossed at the rear of the building and went in the back door of the saloon. The place was empty, everyone out attending the ruckus. He stopped to help himself to a pound of flat-plug chewing tobacco, and a handful of ten-cent cigars. He went out the front door. He mingled with the crowd, staying clear of the wavering torchlight.

"Back, stay clear!" Ox Miller was braying. "We got to block off the street. Wait for him to come out."

The crowd was thinning out. Running for cover. No kidney for a fight. Damn bunch of Yankees and punkin-rollers. By grab, that amount of shooting wouldn't have scared an old-time Forty-Niner crowd very far. Country was taming down, getting soft. He crossed the street, cursing the country and all the people in it.

He was safe for a few seconds in the shadow of a wooden awning, against a rain barrel. So far no one had recognized him, but someone would. He had to lie low. He climbed the rain barrel, reached above, found the wooden rain trough, used it to pull himself to the awning.

He had hoped he could stay there, but it was too narrow, too slanty. He rested on one knee, one hand against the building's false front, and looked at people on the street below. He could have reached down and touched their hats.

He stood, balanced precariously, and got around the edge of the false front to the roof. He climbed the gable. Above him loomed the hotel, Hames's hotel.

Now, thought John, of all the places they *wouldn't* expect him—

He slid down the roof on the other side. He could not see where he was jumping, but he jumped. He lit in ashes and bottles that clanked and crashed. No one paid any attention. No one was here, in this alleyway. He walked to one of the hotel's rear doors, went inside. He was in a hall filled with the smell of cooking. The hall led to the kitchen and the dining room. He wasn't hungry. He came to some narrow stairs, climbed to the second story. He listened to a man's hurried walk along the hall. He didn't want to be recognized, and perhaps have to shoot. He tried the nearest door. It was locked. He started on. A man spoke. The voice came from inside the room. The voice made him stop and come back. He knew who it was—it was Bowden, the old gentleman, Nettie's father.

He rammed the door with his shoulder and the lock gave way, tearing free of the soft pine casing. He was in a dimly lighted room with the arch to a second room beyond. He closed the door and stood listening while the footsteps grew close.

"Who is it?" Bowden asked.

"Hush."

The feet went past without pausing. John went to the draped archway.

"Be ye alone?"

"Yes."

He used the barrel of a Navy to lift the drape. The old man lay in bed, very pale, fumbling, trying to get up.

John looked under the bed; he checked on the window to make sure he couldn't be seen from the street below.

"You!" Bowden said, recognizing him.

"And an improvement on the company ye *been* keeping, I'll wager."

"What was all that shooting? What's happened?"

"Why, they took it in their heads to hang a man, but he war reluctant."

Bowden managed to get out of bed. He stood, holding to the back of a chair. His legs, where they could be seen below his nightgown, were thin as the lower legs of a chicken, or of a grouse, for that's how blue they were.

"We have to get out of here," whispered Bowden, "while he's gone."

"Whilst who's gone?"

"Ed Gaw. He was guarding me. He left when the shooting started, but he'll be—"

"He was holding ye prisoner? For Hames?"

"Yes, but hurry."

"By dang, I'm hurrying for no Ed Gaw." Comanche John was content to rest awhile, give things a chance to cool off. He sat down, tilted his chair back, and put his boots on the bed. "You let your Ed Gaw come if he wants. I'll care for him. Besides, ye got no pants on."

There were no clothes in the room. They waited for Ed Gaw. He was there ten minutes later, a red-faced, stupid-looking man. Finding the latch broken, he stood holding the key, and stared sag-mouthed into the muzzle of the Navy Colt in John's hand.

"Git out of your pants," said John. "The gentleman wants to wear 'em."

They left Gaw gagged and tied to the bed. They could hear drinking in the hotel bar, but the rest of the building was quiet, and it was quiet outside. They probably could have left by the front way, but they didn't. They went around back, and up a side street.

"Only bad thing," said John, watching for pursuit and seeing none, "I lost my horse, but he'll come home, maybe he's home now. And my guns. Got to find my favorite Navies."

"But my daughter—"

"She'll be yonder." He had to help Bowden along; at times he practically carried him; and it was hard going. "Five to one we'll find her in Stumptown."

CHAPTER TWENTY-TWO

NETTIE was at Betsy Cobb's. She was almost as relieved to see John as her father, for she had not led John into a trap—that is, not intentionally, and she told him so over and over.

"Take care of your paw," John said. "For land sakes, gal, how could ye lead me into a trap when ye had no idee I'd be following?"

She helped Betsy Cobb put her father to bed, then they gave him hot tea and rum until he recovered from an attack of the shakes.

Bowden's first words were addressed to Buck Pelton, who came in while this was going on.

"What are you doing *here?*" he asked.

Nettie moved over beside the young man, took his hand, and said, "Dad, we're going to get married."

Bowden lay, looking at them, letting the rum take effect. "I didn't mean that. I mean, why isn't he up on the pass, fighting to save his road? Hames is hauling powder up there by packhorse. He'll blow your trestle to toothpicks. I knew that—that's why he was holding me prisoner, so I couldn't warn you."

Comanche John and Buck Pelton sent for horses and rode off in the early dawn, through intermittent snow. Occasionally, at a distance, they heard the crack of gunfire. At McCabe's first snowshed they met one of the workers coming down, and he told them that the trestle was safe enough, that it still was not controlled by either side, and it was certain that Hames's bunch could not plant powder under it.

"The old gentleman dreamed it up," Buck said, reassured, after his first look at the trestle. "It would be suicide trying to carry powder in there—we'd shoot them like ducks on a pond."

From a vantage point on the road they watched the fight, if it could be called that, with guns at such long

range a man had to arch his bullet ten degrees. To
John's experienced eyes, however, a lot of the shooting
from Hames's side seemed to be just that, shooting for
the sake of shooting, to hear a gun go bang.

John decided to climb for a look at a new angle. He
rode by himself through several rocky turnings. No
road here, only a deer trail. The pass was off to his
left, a U-shaped passage between peaks that towered a
thousand feet higher on either side. The shooting, although farther off, seemed closer than before because
of his elevation, and because of the bare cliff faces
that reflected the sound.

He had to leave his horse behind. He clambered
over huge rocks at the base of the cliff. He crawled
among windfall logs and waded snow to his waist. After a half hour of this, his legs aching from fatigue, he
rounded a flank of the mountain and looked across a
precipitous slope, close to the summit, smooth and
bare of trees, scarred by snow and earth slides of other
seasons. Below, he could see several stretches of the
road, tiny from distance, but not the trestle; it was ob-
scured by the steeper drop of the cliff. In the other direction, up the slope, lay an accumulation of earth,
small rock, and snow. Above this was the summit, a
knob of solid granite.

The accumulation had been undercut and left precariously in place by the snow and earth slides of other years. As he watched, he saw the movements of
men and pack animals near the point of the V. There,
a rough pillar of granite projected through, its key
point, its anchor.

They were preparing to blast it. He could not tell
how far the job had progressed. It would take him an
hour to go below and summon help and argue with
them and convince them and then get back, and an
hour would certainly be too long.

He decided to go on by himself. Damn Pikes Peakers, git in his way anyhow.

One certain thing, however, he couldn't approach

directly across the slope. They would see him and knock him off with a rifle bullet, and anyhow it was too steep, the footing too slippery and friable. He would have to go around.

He retraced his steps, climbed in the protection of the mountain flank, and reached a place of about equal elevation. This time when he came around he had the protection of a dike of rock, a porphyry more resistant to erosion than the rest of the mountain, and hence left to form an uneven wall at most places three or four feet above the surface.

He walked; he crawled, sometimes on hands and knees and sometimes on his stomach, and at last, as the reef commenced to play out, he came up for a look.

He took off his hat and very carefully got his eye to a crevice.

He was now only a long pistol shot away, and he could tell who they were and what they were about.

Three men were unloading a pack mule, doing it very carefully, wary of the explosive they were handling. A fourth man directed them. That was Moose Petley. A fifth stood lookout above the pillar where they were preparing the blast. That was Hames himself. Two other men, whom he had seen from below, had apparently gone around the summit, leading the unloaded mules.

John decided to move just a trifle closer. There was little dike left, at times none at all, but he crawled on his stomach, managing to keep concealed among the larger rocks. To quiet his nerves he muttered to himself:

"What an idee! Slide, accident. Wipe out maybe eighth-mile o' road. Trestle, too. And men. That's why their men are staying clear, far off, not trying to take the trestle. But ye can't tell about a slide. It might jump and do no harm at all. Now, down in Coloraydo . . ."

Down in Coloraydo John had seen some mighty stupendous snowslides. Whole mountains shedding their skins. This wouldn't compare with *them*, but it could be bad enough.

He was so close he could hear the crunch of their boots on rock, he could hear them grunting, saying a few words when need be, mostly saving their breaths.

He peeped again. Moose Petley, still in that buffalo coat, was standing almost atop him, but his side was turned, he was pointing to put this can of powder there, and the other one there, and string the fuse out.

John quietly drew his Navy. Then he cried, "Up your hands! Make a move and you're a dead man!"

A can of powder was dropped. A gun crashed from above. That was Hames. The bullet hit close to John's cheek. It powdered rock and stung him. He dived to a new place, came up with the muzzle of a Navy through a break in the rock, and fired back, but Hames had fallen to his belly.

"Stay where you are!" Hames was shouting. "He's alone. There's *just one man.*"

Someone cried, "Stay and git blasted to Jericho by powder? I'm clearin' out of here."

Hames cursed him and tried to kill him as he ran. He moved along the knob and fired at the spot where John had been. The bullet glanced away with a hornet sound.

"Moose, set the fuse!"

John no longer knew where Moose was.

"He's alone, I tell you, I'll keep him down," called Hames.

Moose answered, "*I'll* keep him down, *you* set the fuse."

It was quiet. John did not know which had decided to touch the fuse, and which had a gun ready to kill him when he showed himself.

He had to move to a new spot. He did it by lying flat on his stomach, boots spread, and pushing himself with first one elbow and then the other.

There were three rocks, forming a little nest. He

could get to one knee there without them seeing him.
He did it.

A trickle of dirt was flowing from above. It had
been loosened by a man's weight. John guessed at the
source of the trickle and raised his head a trifle. He
looked, but no one was there.

"Moose!" shouted Hames.

Hames fired and the bullet flattened itself against
one of the boulders. At the same instant he saw Moose
Petley—on the wrong side.

For a fragment of time John looked down the
round, black muzzle of Moose Petley's gun. He let
himself fall as the gun roared. He was aware of the
flame bursting in his face. He felt the sting of burned
powder and wadding. Concussion deafened him and
seemed to blow the whole side of his head away.

He rolled over. He acted without thinking. There
was a solid place under his feet. He stood and saw Petley and Hames both above him.

He had a flash impression of Moose turning with
drawn pistols, and of Hames in front of the powder-
loaded rock pillar. His own guns and Moose Petley's
guns came in an almost instantaneous roar, but Moose
was hit and his bullets went wild. In that fraction of a
second Hames had taken one running step. He pivoted
with one of his Army pistols drawn. He fired. The bullet whipped wind past John's cheek. Hames was halfway to his knee trying to fan his gun for a second shot,
but there was no time for that. A blast from John's
Navy guns hit him in the middle. He doubled over as
though hit by a sledge. He sat down in the rocks. He
slid, boots out, eyes blank. The slope steepened. He
rolled over and over and kept rolling for a hundred
yards before a mass of snow-filled brush stopped him.
He lay there, doubled over, still, finished.

John breathed and blew. He decided to sit down.
He sat with Navies drawn, getting his wind and
strength. He heard something. He took notice. A hiss
and sputter. And there, above him, was a fuse just

burning itself out of sight into the loaded rock crevice, leaving a black twist of smoke behind it. Hames, then, had lighted it.

He sprang to his feet. Standing, he was seized by indecision whether to run for cover or climb and make an arm's reach for the fuse.

A preliminary spurt of loose powder warned him. He went to his side behind the reef, arms wrapped over his head. Then explosion hit with a force that seemed to jerk the mountain from beneath him.

He was unconscious for perhaps a second. He felt thunder around him. He had no sensation of direction, of up or down. He lay on his stomach, hat under his face, arms around his head as rocks thudded all around. It seemed to last a long time. The thunder faded away. His ears stopped ringing. He gathered his thoughts.

He was still alive. He kept saying over and over that he was still alive. He opened his eyes. He sat up. There was sky above and earth below. The dike was still there and he was clinging to it. The dike had saved him. It had protected him from the explosion and turned the avalanche that followed it.

Above him, everything was changed. The crag was gone, all the tons of earth and rock were gone. He looked for the bodies of Hames and Petley. They had been carried off by the slide. He looked below, and saw the path the slide had taken—a reddish streak through the snow.

Yes, it was like the Gypsy gal had told him. He wasn't fated to hang, or get kilt, but to die in bed, with his boots off and his guns hung on the bedpost.

He rested and got his bearings, and finally he went below and caught his horse and rode around to see what had happened to the road.

Upflung strata of a resistant quartzite rock had deflected the slide somewhat, channeling it down through that same old cut where Nealy had had all his trouble, and the road was gone for a distance, but it wasn't bad, only a couple days more of building.

He could hear a lot of distant talking and shouting back and forth. Someone had been killed. "Smith," he pondered, "Smith." Why, that was *him*.

Comanche John thought about it. It gave him a good, free feeling not to worry about hangropes, or have the responsibility of being a big businessman, a freight-line operator. He rode the mountain by himself and took notice of what a fine day it was for November. Cold, but with a good gray-blue sky, and how fine and purplish the forest looked, especially to the nor'east, in the land of the Blackfeet.

He tried out a chaw of the store tobacco. He spent the day at his ease, slowly descending, and at dark he had made up his mind.

There was a light in the Widow's cabin, and Stocker's wagon was hitched in front. They'd be talking, Stocker and his missus and the Widow, and they were noisy talkers, so there was nothing to prevent him slipping into the back door for just a snack.

He got inside without incident.

It was dark, with only a little light coming over the three-quarters partition that divided the house, and he sort of smelled his way, finding some cold hardpan bread, a piece of jerked venison, tea, a string of some of the Widow's secret-recipe smoked trout, and he found a pan to do some cooking in. He took an old blanket, too, and rolled his things in it, making a wolf pack. Then he was ready to go, but the Widow was talking about him, so he listened.

". . . And he was standing there, right by the boot-jack, not more'n twelve hours ago, and I talked sharp to him about tracking his wet jackboots all over my floor. And those were my last words to him. Oh, I wish I could take those words back, but I can't, no, I'll never git a chance to in this world."

Why, said John to himself, *the poor woman's crying.*

Mrs. Stocker said, "Now don't you chide yourself, Sister Cobb, a woman's got to talk that way to her menfolk or else—"

"I drove him out, and it war for the last time. And the way he *looked* at me, with that peculiar smile on his face, sort of far away, as if he could see into the future, as if he *knowed*. Like he had inner sight. Things like that happen, you know. It comes to folks in a flash. And now he's dead and cold and I'll never see him any more."

Comanche John wiped a tear from the corner of his eye.

"No," the Widow was saying, "I'll never see him this side o' Beulah Land. When I think of him cut down in his prime, in the flower of his manhood—"

Stocker said, "I'd say he was a mite gone to seed."

"In the flower of his manhood! Who are *you* to talk agin' him, *you* that wanted to hang him over at Big Hole?"

Comanche John did a dance, whacking his pants legs silently, whispering, "Give it to him, Widda!"

"Don't you talk agin' my John. It may be he used strong language betimes, and he scratched, though why I never determined, and I suspected him of strong drink, but he was religious. Yes, I do believe he was saved."

John was tempted to step out from behind the partition and gladden her heart as it had never been gladdened before. But she was talking and he decided to wait for just a moment.

"Anyhow, why'd he have bad habits? I'll tell you— because he lacked advantages. Well, I'd have *given* him advantages. I'd have broke him of chewing and scratching and cursing and all the rest, I would. I'd have done it with kindness, and if that didn't work I'd have beaten 'em out of him with the stove tongs. I'd have got him shaved and dressed up, and you wouldn't have known him."

Comanche John decided not to gladden her after all. He picked up the wolf pack with one hand and groped for the door with the other. He could hear her saying, "I do wish you'd see if you couldn't get a hearse here from Last Chance. I know it'd be expen-sive, but I think we should do it. And plumes. It would soften the blow if we had plumes. And see if you can't find the body. Laws, what good's a hearse without the body? Yes, you must find it, we *can't* have a respectable funeral without the body. I got my mind so set on . . ."

Comanche John softly closed the door. His gunpowder pony was in the horse corral like he hoped it would be. And his old saddle. All was quiet, no watchman, only the teamsters drinking trade likker and arguing over a game of seven-up.

He rode down the gulch and across a ridge, and the last light of Stumptown was gone from sight, but below, to his left, he could see the road that led to the New York Bar, and the Three Forks, and Confederate Gulch, and the Hooraw Diggings, and after that the wild land of the Blackfeet.

He breathed deeply, and took off his slouch hat, and let the wind blow through his tangled long hair.

"That woman!" he muttered. "I'm going to stay clear of that woman. She always *did* want to bury me."

He felt better with a mile between them, and better still with two, and at three he was singing:

> *"The yaller gold came easy,*
> *And he spent it just as free;*
> *He always chawed tobacker*
> *Wherever he might be."*

Dan Cushman was born in Osceola, Michigan, and grew up on the Cree Indian reservation in Montana. He graduated from the University of Montana with a Bachelor of Science degree in 1934 and pursued a career in mining as a prospector, assayer, and geologist before turning to journalism. In the early 1940s his novelette-length stories began appearing regularly in such Fiction House magazines as *North-West Romances* and *Frontier Stories*. Later in the decade his North-Western and Western stories as well as fiction set in the Far East and Africa began appearing in *Action Stories, Adventure,* and *Short Stories.* A collection of some of his best North-Western and Western fiction has recently been published, *Voyageurs of the Midnight Sun* (1995), with a Foreword by John Jakes who cites Cushman as a major influence in his own work. The character Comanche John, a Montana road agent featured in numerous rollicking magazine adventures, also appears in Cushman's first novel, *Montana, Here I Be* (1950) and in two later novels. *Stay Away, Joe,* which first appeared in 1953, is an amusing novel about the mixture, and occasional collision, of Indian culture and Anglo-American culture among the Métis (French Indians) living on a reservation in Montana. The novel became a bestseller and remains a classic to this day, greatly loved especially by Indian peoples for its truthfulness and humor. Yet, while humor became Cushman's hallmark in such later novels as *The Old Copper Collar* (1957) and *Goodbye, Old Dry* (1959), he also produced significant historical fiction in *The Silver Mountain* (1957), concerned with the mining and politics of silver in Montana in the 1890s. This novel won a Gold Spur Award from the Western Writers of America. His fiction remains notable for its breadth, ranging all the way from a story of the cattle frontier in *Tall Wyoming* (1957) to a poignant and memorable portrait of small town life in Michigan just before the Great War in *The Grand and the Glorious* (1963). More recent fiction such as *Rusty Irons* (1984) combines both the humor for which he is best known and the darker hues to be found in *The Silver Mountain.* His most recent novels are *In Alaska With Shipwreck Kelly* (1995) and *Valley of the Thousand Smokes* (1996).